GRAY'S DOMAIN

THE PURGATORIUM, BOOK TWO

Eva Pohler

Eva Pohler Books
20011 Park Ranch
San Antonio, Texas 78259
www.evapohler.com

Publisher's Note: This is a work of fiction. Names, characters, places, and incidents are a product of the author's imagination. Locales and public names are sometimes used for atmospheric purposes. Any resemblance to actual people, living or dead, or to businesses, companies, events, institutions, or locales is completely coincidental.

Book Layout ©2017 BookDesignTemplates.com

Book Cover Design by Wydawnictwo Replika

Gray's Domain/ Eva Pohler. -- 1st ed.
Paperback ISBN: 978-1-958390-52-8

It's not why, but what.

—HORTENSE GRAY

Contents

For my family.

Ghosts

Daphne Janus left her unit at Santa Cruz Island Resort, crept past the abandoned pool glowing in the darkness, and made her way down the sidewalk beyond the other cabanas. The wind blew heavily tonight, and she pulled the hoodie further down over her eyes—not because it was cold out, but because she did not want her bald head exposed. She stifled a giggle as she reached Brock's unit and knocked on the door.

The door opened, and there was Brock, in a white t-shirt and boxers and with mussed up hair and puffy eyes, looking as sexy as ever. "Daph?"

"I'm scared. Can I come in?"

He blinked. "Of course."

He opened the door wider, and she slipped by, trying not to laugh.

"I'm surprised you're talking to me." He ran a hand through his dark, unruly hair, which only further reminded her that her own was gone.

But enough self-pity. It angered her that he looked so hot with bed-head and sleepy blue eyes. She fought the urge to kiss him.

"I heard strange noises outside my room," she lied. "Can I sleep here tonight?"

He placed his hand over his heart, like he was about to recite *The Pledge of Allegiance.* "Does this mean you forgive me?"

Absolutely not, she thought. "I think so."

He stepped closer and touched his lips to hers. His lips were soft and thick and felt good, but the memory of what he'd done to her over the past couple of days, making her believe he was on her side, brought the clarity she needed to resist. She bit down hard on his bottom lip.

"Ow!" He flinched back, hands rushing to his mouth. "I guess I deserved that."

And so much more, she thought. *But don't worry. Payback is coming.*

"I'm sorry." She sat on the edge of the bed and stared at her lap. "I have mixed feelings about everything. I know you were only trying to help, but..."

He sat beside her, not quite touching her, and licked the blood from his lip. "I know." Without looking at her, he said, "The whole time I was doing it, I wasn't sure. Dr. Gray made it seem right."

She rubbed her thighs, suddenly chilled beneath her sweats. Brock had meant her no harm. He had wanted to help her. She was wrong to deceive him back. But wasn't *she* helping *him* now? It was revenge, but it was also therapy. "I just wish I could know for sure how much of it was real."

He lifted her chin and gazed into her eyes. "Everything about how I feel—all of that was real. Please say you believe me. It'll kill me if you don't."

Payback didn't look so good anymore. "Oh, Brock."

He kissed her again, taking her in his arms. His mouth tasted like mint with a hint of blood, and his hair smelled clean and musky. The muscles in his chest and shoulders enveloped her, exciting her. He pressed her down on the bed as tears sprang to her eyes. She clutched the hood to keep it from revealing her head. That's all it took—the memory of her hair being shaved while he did nothing to stop it—to call up her anger.

He reached his hand to her bare scalp, but she pulled away.

"Don't," she said.

"You're still beautiful, you know."

"I don't feel beautiful." She sat up on the edge of the bed.

He sat up beside her, not quite touching her again. "But do you think this place helped you?"

As mad as she was at all of them for tricking her in such a cruel way—making her think she was in danger, terrifying her into running for her life—she had to admit she no longer felt like the pitiful girl she was a week ago. She wasn't sure, though, if her feelings of self-loathing and guilt hadn't simply been replaced by a need for revenge. Once she put her parents and Brock through the same terrifying torture as they had put her, would the self-loathing return?

"I think so," she finally said.

"It'll probably take time to know for sure."

She didn't like how nice he was being to her.

He covered her hand with his. "I want to be there for you, Daph. Please don't shut me out again."

Then a loud knock on the door made her jump. The ghosts, she thought.

"Who else would be knocking this late?" Brock crossed the room to the door.

She shrugged and shook her head, the thrill of the game making her tremble with excitement. She felt on the verge of hysteria as she waited for him to open the door.

He peered through one of the front windows. "I can't tell who's there, but it looks like a group of kids."

The door burst open. Brock moved between the intruders and Daphne. Five of them stood in the doorway with their faces and clothes covered in white powder. Red goo dripped from red eyes and blue lips.

"What's going on?" Brock held his arms out like a shield between the ghosts and Daphne.

"Are you one of the living or the dead?" a ghost boy, probably Dave, asked in a low growl.

"What the hell? Get out! Do you know what time it is?" Brock charged them, but before he reached them, a turbo-sized water gun sprayed white powder all over him. He rushed his hands to his face, shouting obscenities.

Daphne jumped from the bed, eager to play along. That's when a pale hand wrapped itself around her wrist and dragged her from the room.

"Come with us," one of the ghosts, whom she now recognized as Cam, whispered quickly at her ear. "Pretend we're abducting you."

He had his black hood pulled low over his eyes, making him unrecognizable. Her parents, whom he had helped torment about an hour ago, hadn't recognized Cam either. She had watched from behind a shrub through the window of their unit as the ghosts played their mischief on her parents. Another giggle escaped her throat as she recalled the high she had felt then—the same high she felt now.

Her cheeks stretched wide. "Love it."

"Let's make a run for it," he whispered. "The others will hold him back."

She and Cam sprinted past the pool toward the boardwalk. At this late hour, well after midnight, no one else roamed the sidewalks of the resort. Even Gregory and Emma had left the poolside where they had been making out earlier in the evening. The place felt abandoned. Only a few lights on the third floor of the main building showed signs of life.

"Daphne?" Brock cried from the room.

"We're taking her with us!" one of the ghosts—Bridget—said as Daphne raced away.

"Daphne!" Brock called again.

When Daphne and Cam reached the boardwalk, Daphne shouted at the top of her lungs, not sure if he would hear her, "Brock! Help! These people are crazy!"

She smiled gleefully and followed Cam, her heart pumping as she skipped down the wooden steps to the sand, where the moonlight illuminated the sea.

"Lie down here on the beach while the rest of us hide in the shadows," Cam instructed. "We'll ambush the both of you. You play the terrified victim, 'kay?"

"Got it."

He squeezed her hand. "You okay?"

She nodded, not sure what he meant. Physically, she felt great. And at the moment, she felt exuberant, never better.

He kissed her cheek and dashed away.

Two other ghosts joined Cam in the shadows of the bluffs as Daphne lay on her back on the cool sand by the shore. The moon was waning but still nearly full, and the stars were brilliant in a cloudless sky. The breeze off the sea chilled her.

Turning toward the boardwalk, she screamed in the otherwise quiet night, "Brock! Help me!"

Brock soon appeared on the top of the boardwalk, followed by the last two ghosts—Stan and Dave—who must have held him back.

Again, she screamed, "Brock! I'm down here!"

He rushed down the steps and knelt at her side.

"What happened? Are you okay?"

Before she could answer, all five ghosts surrounded them, chanting, "You are not living! You are the dead! You are not living! You are the dead!"

Brock shoved the actors down on the sand, scooped Daphne into his arms, and raced up the wooden steps toward the resort. She could feel his heart hammering in his chest against her, his breath pumping hard as it was sucked in and out. A thrill moved through her. Even though she knew this was all an act, it was nevertheless titillating. At the top of the steps, Brock looked back at the ghosts, who were no longer following them but had disappeared in the shadows.

"This is bullshit," he said, along with a few other choice words. "Are you okay? Can you walk?"

"I think so."

He set her on her feet and then pressed his hands to his knees, trying to catch his breath.

"Thanks for coming to my rescue." She tried to sound spooked.

"What the hell just happened?" he asked her as he led her back to his room, holding tightly to her hand. "Did they hurt you?"

"No. They just scared me, that's all." She dusted sand from her bottom. "You don't think they were real ghosts, do you?"

"Of course not, but I thought the games were over. I've had enough."

She wanted to say, *So it's not so fun being on the other side*, but she held her tongue because, for one thing, she couldn't let him know how she really felt, and, for another, because she knew from experience, that despite his anger, a part of him had found the experience as thrilling as she.

The door to his room was ajar, so he went in first, turned on more lights, and checked around before motioning Daphne inside. She avoided his eyes, finding it hard not to laugh. She wanted to jump up and down and exhibit the feelings of excitement that were building up inside her, but she pretended to be frightened and shaken by the experience. Brock locked the door and pulled one of the chairs against it as she and her parents had both done before him, while she covered her face with her hands and tried to get a grip on her feelings. All she could think was how much she couldn't wait for the next game to begin.

A half hour later, after she and Brock had taken turns in the shower, she lay in clean borrowed clothes in Brock's arms biting her lips to keep from giggling. She could only imagine how much fun the next few days would be. She wondered what Hortense had in store for Brock and her parents. Would they get stuck in a dark elevator like she had with Stan?

Would their kayak group get trapped with Hairy Larry in a sea cave by the tide? Would they be bucked off their horses during their trail ride with Kelly and get lost on the haunted side of the island?

This last thought upset her. Although she wanted to frighten her parents and Brock, she didn't want them to get hurt. She could have been killed falling off of the horse. Ironically, that was what she had hoped for when she had agreed to come with Cam to this island. She'd wanted to die. It seemed like such a long time ago. She recalled kneeling in the stream in Central Valley after escaping from Stan and Larry, and then lying on her back, like the woman in the painting in Hortense's office. The thought of taking her life now seemed stupid.

She still regretted not getting up that night her brother went to her sister's room, and in his sickness, attempted to strangle a demon from their sister's body. She still believed she might have changed the outcome of that terrible moment if she had gone into Kara's room when she was awakened by the thumping sound, but she now understood she hadn't caused Kara's death. She wasn't responsible. Her brother, Joey, was sick. Hortense Gray's strange therapeutic games had forced her to face the truth: she was helpless against the past. It was immutable—the word Hortense had used, meaning unchangeable. Taking her life would solve nothing.

If she had her poetry journal, she would write:

Today is another day
And tomorrow, too;
And though I miss your sweet voice
You're in everything I do.

She wanted her parents and Brock to benefit from Hortense Gray's therapy, but she wouldn't allow their lives to be risked in the same way. As she lay there composing poetry and listening to Brock's steady breathing beside her, she decided she would visit Hortense in the morning and make sure no rough play was part of the games.

First she'd have to convince her parents and Brock to stay. After their encounter with the ghosts, they sounded determined to leave. Daphne couldn't let that happen. She had way too much to look forward to in the form of their torment to let them leave now.

In the morning, Daphne awoke before Brock. She snuck out to take another shower and dress in her room. She put on the scarf her mother had brought, and the fact that her mother had known to bring it renewed her anger and need for revenge. She decided to give her parents a call and ask them to meet her for breakfast. She used her friendliest voice. Her father sounded shocked but agreed.

Up in the third-floor banquet hall, she spotted her parents sitting together at a table by themselves, avoiding eye contact with the other people, who were going back and forth from the breakfast buffet to their seats. Both her parents wore khaki shorts and light-colored button-down shirts. Her mother wore her frosted hair pulled back in the thick brown headband that had become her staple accessory. She suddenly looked small and fragile sitting there next to Daphne's father. Daphne also spotted Cam, Emma, Gregory, Pete, and Stan sitting with Hortense, fawning over the doctor like they all had school-girl crushes, all wearing silver bracelets exactly like the one on Daphne's wrist. They gave Daphne friendly waves, and she nodded to them in return, still feeling ambivalent about their roles in her torment. Brock was nowhere in sight. She frowned and worried she should have called him and told him she'd meet him here, too.

Her parents looked up at her when she approached their table.

"Can I sit with you?" she asked.

"Of course," her mother said, her brows in a v. "You don't have to ask."

She noticed they had waited for her before making their plates. "Let's go get some grub, then."

As they filled their plates with eggs, hash browns, fruit, and muffins, her father warned her that they planned to leave as soon as possible.

"But this place is helping me," Daphne said, which wasn't a lie. "I want to finish the therapy."

Her parents exchanged looks of surprise, and when they returned to their table to eat, her father said, "Well, that's good to hear, Daph. An absolute relief."

Daphne noticed tears brimming in his eyes, and she flooded with guilt over what she planned to do to them.

"We'll stay as planned, then," her mother said, pulling the scarf a little further down on Daphne's head.

Daphne flinched from her mother's touch, causing her mother to frown and look away, down at her plate.

"I'm sorry," Daphne muttered. She hadn't realized how angry she still felt toward her mother. She had so many feelings bottled inside of her, and for some reason, most of the negative ones were brought on by her mother.

Maybe it was because she had said those words that continued to haunt Daphne: "You mean you heard and did nothing?"

Daphne had wanted to die then. She had wanted to curl up in a ball and die.

The past is immutable, she reminded herself as she twirled the silver bracelet on her wrist. *We can only learn to live with it.*

As they ate, she listened to her parents recount what had happened the night before with the ghosts. Daphne fought hard not to smile, especially at her mother's exaggerations—there were ten or twenty? They were all over six feet tall? Before they had finished eating, though, Hortense appeared beside their table, looming over Daphne like an evil spirit. *No, like Prospero.*

"I need to speak with you privately in my office," she said to Daphne. "Please come by when you're finished." Then she looked at Daphne's parents, gave them a curt nod, and left the dining hall.

CHAPTER TWO

Fear Profiles

Daphne sat in the green chenille chair across from Hortense Gray's messy desk in an office overflowing with paintings, books, sculptures, a loom, and an upright piano. Hortense was just now closing the lid on her old-fashioned record player, which was plunked on one side of her desk. She wore a strange smile.

"I'm pleased you decided to stay," Hortense said, sitting back in her high-back leather chair behind the desk. "You've had a taste of how things work on the other side, I presume?"

Daphne nodded, unable to prevent the smile from crossing her face.

"Good. Very good. I'm glad to hear that." The doctor shuffled a few papers around on her desk and opened a file. "I asked you here because we need to discuss the fear profiles for your parents and Brock."

"Fear profiles?"

"Of course. I'm sure you've realized by now it was no coincidence that your therapeutic games played on your worst fears."

"That wasn't hard to figure out."

"Your parents and Cam gave me the information I needed to set up the games." Hortense cleared her throat. "Now I need information from you to design therapy tailored to your parents and Brock. Let's start with your father." She sat up and picked up a pen. "What would you say is his worst fear?"

Daphne thought about that. "Well, you can't use his very worst one, because that's helicopters."

"Of course, we can. Arturo Gomez travels in his private helicopter on and off the island all the time. He would be thrilled if we incorporated it into an exercise." Hortense leaned forward. "But tell me, what exactly about helicopters frightens your father? And do you have any idea why?"

"I think it's called PTSD or something? My dad was in the military."

"Is that right?" Hortense asked. "Did he see any action?"

"In the Gulf War. He never talks about it. I only know because my mother told me."

"So, your mother told you he doesn't like helicopters? He never told you himself?"

"A long time ago, when I was little, we went on a cruise, and I wanted to go on a helicopter ride at one of the ports. I was kind of a brat about it, so Mother pulled me aside and told me that they make my dad really, really sick. That's all I know."

Hortense wrote something down in her file, nodding. "That's helpful information."

"You don't think that would be too much for him, do you?" Daphne asked.

"It will be good for him. Trust me." Hortense made another note. "What other fears does your father possess? Heights? Blood? Spiders?"

Daphne shook her head. "He's not afraid of any of those things. I really can't think of anything else except..." Daphne stopped, unsure if she should reveal what had popped into her head.

The doctor looked across her desk at her. "Except what?"

Daphne sucked in her lips and shrugged.

The doctor smiled. "Except losing you. Isn't that what you were about to say?"

Daphne nodded, feeling the blood rush to her face. Was she so transparent?

"That goes without saying," Hortense said. "It doesn't take a psychologist to see that both of your parents, and even Brock, fear your death more than anything else, even the loss of their own lives."

Daphne's mouth dropped open. "I wouldn't say that. I don't think…"

"It's obvious you don't think your mother and Brock love you with the same intensity as your father."

"That's not true," Daphne replied automatically. It couldn't be true, could it? Now she began to wonder if maybe it was. Maybe she *could* admit it now. She always felt that her dad loved her more than anyone else.

Hortense gave her a patronizing smile and said, "Let's move on to your mother."

"My mother is easier. She doesn't like the outdoors and is afraid of just about anything small that crawls—spiders, bugs, lizards."

"Oh?"

"They don't even have to be dangerous or poisonous. Even roaches have her running and screaming across the room."

"That does sound easy."

"Once, there was a lizard on the wall in her bathroom, and she wouldn't take a shower until my dad caught it and proved it was out of the room."

Hortense chuckled. "Sounds fun already." She made a note in her file. "Anything else?"

Daphne thought for a moment. "Horses. She won't ride them. I don't know why. When we went to Colorado a long time ago, she wouldn't go with the rest of us on a trail ride."

Hortense made another note and said, "Very good. What about Brock?"

"I don't think he's afraid of anything."

"There's got to be something. Everyone's afraid of something. Think, Daphne."

Daphne gnawed on the inside of her bottom lip, trying to recall any-thing, any little thing. He wasn't afraid of small spaces, as he proved when he climbed into the tiny car of a carnival ride one night at the Po-teet Fair as she watched from below. That same night, he proved he wasn't afraid of heights as he held her trembling body on the Ferris wheel while he shouted, "Woo, hoo!" He'd flown several times for na-tionals in swimming and seemed to have no issues with airplanes. Bugs didn't bother him. Elevators didn't bother him, even though he always took the stairs if she didn't feel up to riding. He drove the speed limit but wasn't afraid of reckless driving either, as he'd proved to her once on a Malibu go-cart racetrack. Then she recalled one of many days they'd visited the pet store. He loved checking out the dogs and was trying to decide which breed of dog he most preferred. Not long after they broke up, he bought a Bernese Mountain Dog. Once, while they were visiting the pet store, she'd wanted to hold a snake, and he'd re-fused to even come near one.

"Snakes! I'd forgotten about that. He says they creep him out. I don't know if it's *that* big of a fear, but it's all I can think of."

"We've used snakes in our therapy many times, so that's no problem. Can you think of anything else?"

Daphne shook her head. Then she remembered what she'd wanted to say to Hortense. "But I have something else I want to say."

"What is it?"

"Please don't put my parents and Brock in any real danger. When I was bucked off that horse…"

"That was an accident."

"But still…"

"There's always some risk involved in any kind of therapy. The risks here might be greater than those in the traditional clinic, but the success rate can't even be touched by conventional means."

"Yeah, but…"

"Look, any time a doctor prescribes a drug, most drugs have side ef-fects and even harmful effects, but when the good outweighs the harm, the doctor writes the prescription."

Daphne frowned. She could have *died.* "Some risks are greater than others. Maybe horses are too unpredictable."

"Not true. We've been using horses for ten years. Pearl is trained to run directly to Stan's camp. You are the very first to have been bucked off before she completed her mission. The odds are still too good."

"What if I would have died?"

Hortense frowned. "You didn't."

"Maybe the fact that Kelly had been away on maternity leave…"

Hortense nodded. "Maybe so. In any case, she's been working with the horses every day since. I don't anticipate any more surprises."

They were silent as Hortense made a few more notes in her file. Daphne gazed around the room, studying all the art. The painting of the girl about to lie down on her back in the stream was now up on the wall crammed between two other paintings of different styles. This reminded Daphne of her last visit to the Dr. Gray's office and of the article she had found in *The Tempest.*

"I finished *The Tempest,* by the way," Daphne said, studying the doc-tor's response. "I need to return it to you."

"I told you to keep it."

"There was something folded inside that I think you might want back." Daphne's heart raced.

"Oh? What was it?"

"A newspaper article about you."

The doctor's face drained of color. "Did you read it?"

Daphne nodded. "And I was wondering…"

"Yes?"

Daphne's mouth went dry. "Did your father give you your scars?"

The doctor closed her file and folded her arms across her chest. "My father was a great man."

Daphne looked at her lap, embarrassed for having asked the question. She wanted to run from the room. "I'm sorry."

"No need to apologize. You're a curious child. That's a positive trait. Maybe one day, you'll consider the field of psychology. You have the mind for it."

Daphne looked up in surprise. She hadn't expected praise. "Thank you."

"Do you have any further questions for me?"

"No ma'am…except when will the games begin? And how will I know what to do?"

"Cameron will help you through them. And remember, the exercises are as much *art* as they are *science*. Part of my concept of living art is that the games are not scripted. I want you to improvise, be spontaneous. There is no right or wrong in this, okay?"

That was a relief. "Thank you, doctor."

"You're quite welcome. Thanks for your cooperation."

Daphne took this as a dismissal, so she stood up and crossed the room to the door.

"Daphne?"

"Yes?" She stopped at the door and turned to face Dr. Gray.

"The only mistake you can make is to break the illusion. Under no circumstances should you warn your parents or Brock that none of it is real. In many ways, the games are as real as our experiences in the outside world, and a sudden breach in the illusion could ruin the therapy for all involved. Understood?"

"Yes, ma'am."

On her way back to her room from Hortense Gray's office, Daphne noticed the young group she had come to think of as "the regulars," which included Emma, Gregory, Stan, Vince, Dave, Bridget, and Cam—though Cam wasn't with them at the moment. They stood at the edge of the pool still wearing their clothes from breakfast and were cheering on a race. Dave, the loudest and rowdiest of the group, was shouting Cam's name. She ran over to join them and peered into the pool to see Cam racing Brock, who was a full length ahead of him.

"Hey, kiddo!" Stan greeted her as she moved beside him. He patted her back and said, "Cam is getting creamed by your boyfriend."

"Well, Brock *is* a competitive swimmer," Daphne said. "He's hard to beat."

Daphne was surprised when Bridget took her by the elbow and said, "So how did you like last night? Thrilling, wasn't it?"

Daphne gave her a smile and a nod. "Actually, yes."

"Just wait," Bridget said. "It gets even better."

"Come on, Cam!" Dave howled. "You're pathetic!"

Vince covered his mouth and giggled.

"What are you laughing at?" Dave teased. Then he shoved Vince into the pool, soaking him, clothes and all.

The other regulars busted out laughing.

Vince popped up with a smile and pointed at Dave. "This isn't over."

Everyone laughed again. Then Cam pulled himself up on the deck, panting for air.

"Oh, God," he said between breaths. "Brock's killing me."

Dave extended a hand to Vince, who tried to pull him in but failed. Dave easily lifted the skinny Vince out of the water, and at that moment, Daphne realized the two boys were lovers—something in the way they looked at one another.

Brock was still swimming, unaware that the race was over.

"Should we leave him there?" Emma said in a soft voice. "Sneak away and let him figure it out?"

The group agreed, and all but Cam and Daphne left the pool area, going in different directions.

Daphne found a towel neatly folded on a nearby lounger and handed it to Cam.

"I think that's Brock's," Cam said. "He was swimming laps before I got here. I can't believe he's still going."

"It's what he does. Here. Take it. He won't mind. It'll probably be dry by the time he's done."

Cam took the towel and rubbed it through his hair. "Listen. There's a new boy here, a sixteen-year-old."

"Here for therapy?"

"Yeah. So, if I say something—I don't know—strange sounding, just go with it, okay?"

Daphne looked at him sideways. "How strange sounding?"

"Just be ready to improvise. He's had a rough time. Dr. Gray says he keeps his emotions suppressed—won't face them—and it's up to us to help bring them to the surface."

"What happened to him?"

"His mom abandoned him when he was five. It took the state two years to track down his dad, but the dad didn't want him. Then he was abused by a foster father for, like, three years. Apparently he was in a good home after that for two years, but when the mother died of cancer, the foster dad checked out and returned the kid to the state. A wealthy family adopted him, and after trying everything else to help him with his drug problem, they sent him here."

"Poor guy."

"Yeah. He's pretty bad off."

"What's his name?"

"Giovanni."

Daphne turned the silver bracelet around and around her left wrist. Then she asked, "Are you sure scaring the crap out of him is best?"

"Absolutely."

As they each sat on a lounger to wait for Brock, Daphne asked, "Are Vince and Dave a couple?"

Cam frowned. "They don't want anyone to know, but everyone does. We just can't let Vince's dad find out."

"It shouldn't be hard here on the island."

"Oh, but it is. Vince's dad is Dr. Reynolds."

"Seriously?" She hadn't seen that coming—though now that she thought about it, they were both tall, thin, and quiet.

"He's nice enough, but he doesn't pay much attention to Vince—in my opinion, anyway. And I've seen him lose it—berate Vince in front of everybody. I think Lee is in love with Hortense and doesn't really care about anything else."

Daphne was about to ask more when Brock climbed from the pool and snatched his towel from Cam's hands.

"You mind?" Brock asked.

Cam laughed. "Sorry, man."

"No worries."

After pondering the new information about the regulars, Daphne was brought back to her senses by the sound of a helicopter above them.

All three of them turned their faces toward the sky, but only one of them couldn't stop herself from smiling.

CHAPTER THREE

Bird Trail

Later that morning, Roger drove Daphne and her parents up the canyon ridge to Prisoners Harbor, where the bird hiking trail began near the pier. On the way, Daphne sat beside Roger in the front of the jeep, and twice, he turned his eyes to hers and gave her a conspiratorial wink. As excited as Daphne was about the impending game, she was also nervous and a little frightened, because she didn't know what was coming. She only knew what she had shared with Hortense about her parents' fears. No script or preparation had been given to her. Her only instructions were to play along and to never break the illusion. She hoped she wouldn't mess up and give the game away. She bit the inside of her lip, psyching herself up to be brave, serious, and strong.

As they passed Central Valley, Daphne shuddered in spite of its lush, grassy knolls, sparkling stream, and purple mountain glory, because she was reminded of what, just days ago, she'd almost done. Again that seemed so long ago and so very stupid to her now, but the memory of pressing her face into the stream and waiting for her lungs to burn was still fresh and biting.

The jeep wound along the canyon ridge and up to the peak above Prisoners Harbor, where it came to a stop beneath a scraggily tree and a series of picnic tables. A wooden outhouse and kayak rental were just past the tree toward the pier, and out in the harbor were hundreds of boats. As they climbed from the jeep with the binoculars Roger had given them, they turned in the direction of the squawking pelicans.

"Look at them all," Daphne said, pointing down to the harbor. "Aren't they amazing?"

Her father fixed his binoculars on them. "Sure are. I'd like to get a picture once we get a little closer."

"You brought your camera?" Daphne asked.

"'Course I did."

She hoped he hadn't taken any photos of the Limuw ritual. Just the possibility of this renewed her need to get revenge.

Roger took off his white straw cowboy hat and waved it toward the pier. "You can see the large population of pelicans in Pelican Bay, and as we move along this ridge toward the trailhead, scan farther east for other coastline species."

"Like what?" Daphne's mother, Sharon, asked.

Roger ran a hand through his graying hair before returning the hat to his head. "For example, over there, all by its lonesome, see that big white bird?" Roger pointed to a jetty west of the pelicans. "That there's the great egret." A pair of gulls flew overhead. "And the gulls are all over the place. Sometimes you'll see blue herons, too."

They followed Roger down the hill toward the pier.

"Don't forget the bald eagle," Daphne added.

"That's a rare sight," Roger said. "And usually in Central Valley."

"What about those black birds over there?" her dad asked, pointing to a pair at the very edge of the shoreline.

"Them there are black oyster catchers. They mostly nest in the gravely shoreline on this side of the island. I'm glad you got to see 'em, 'cause you won't see 'em where I'm taking you now, in the woods. That's where the rare birds are."

Roger led them to the west of the pier down a trail that ran parallel to the shore but farther inland, through a belt of oaks. Daphne had not yet explored this part of the island, except in a kayak along the shoreline, and was surprised by the shade trees. With the exception of the ancient oak on the other side of the island near Bowen Point and the woodsy area near the naval tower, she'd not seen trees tall and full enough to make decent shade.

As Roger led them into the woods, he said in a hushed voice, "This here is the best place to spot the island scrub jay. They fly all over the island, but they like to nest in these trees. And the Channel Islands are the only places in the whole world where you can find them. Keep your voices down so as not to scare 'em away. You're bound to see other rare beauties here, too, like the pigeon guillemot. You can tell it from other birds by its red feet. It's black with a white patch on its wings and pretty rare." As they followed him beneath the oaks, he added, "But the rarest of all are xantus's murrelets. There's a cave past these woods where they're known to nest. We'll check it out."

He turned to Daphne and gave her another wink. She took this to mean something was going to happen in the cave. A surge of adrenaline moved through her. She wished Brock hadn't opted to nap in his room. She would have loved to see his reaction to whatever was coming.

As they hiked down the trail, Roger pointed out a number of birds, including two island scrub jays, which Daphne's dad successfully captured in a photo. Although the trees shaded Daphne and her fellow hikers from the heat of the sun, there was less of a breeze, making the air muggy and hot. Daphne frequently stopped to sip from her water bottle. The scarf on her head only added to the heat, but she didn't dare take it off. She hated the way she looked without her long, brown hair.

Soon they came to a rocky cave. Daphne's heart rate increased with anticipation. She hoped she wasn't expected to go inside. Why would Hortense design an exercise that pushed Daphne out of *her* comfort zone? Daphne's therapy was over.

Roger stopped the group and waved them in closer to him, where he spoke in a quiet voice.

"As I said, xantus's murrelet is one of the rarest endangered birds in the world. People come from all over to spot them on this here island." He took off his straw cowboy hat and fanned his face. "This cave is known to have some, and believe me, they never leave their nests except at night. Thing is, we gotta be careful not to disturb them, on the count of 'em being so rare."

"I guess that means no pictures," Joe said.

"That's right. No pictures 'cause the flash will scare 'em. No talking. You can take a long look as long as you stay real still. I'll go in with each one of you, one at a time, and show you the nests with my flashlight. There were two nests in there last week." He returned his hat to his head and looked around at them. "Who wants to go first?"

"Not me," Daphne said.

"Joe, you go," Sharon said.

Daphne felt her heart pounding with anticipation. She wondered what would really be inside the cave. Her body tensed. *She* was not going into the cave, no matter what.

As Roger led her dad through the three-foot-by-three-foot opening, she and her mother exchanged worried glances. Why was her mother worried?

Her mother said, "You don't have to go in if you're not up to it, Daph."

Daphne shrugged. "I can probably do it, but you go first, okay?"

Her mother gave her a gentle smile. "It's been nice, spending time out here with you today." Tears formed in the corners of Sharon's eyes and her fingers trembled as she adjusted the wide headband holding back her frosted hair. "It's been too long, Honey."

Daphne looked at her sneakers as the warmth rushed to her already hot face.

"Have you forgiven us, then?" her mother asked.

"I'm working on it," Daphne answered truthfully.

Her mother patted her shoulder and said, "That's good to hear, sweetheart."

Daphne choked back the lump in her throat and pretended to be interested in something above them in the trees.

Soon Roger and Joe crept from the cave. When they were far enough away from the entrance, Joe said, "They're incredible. Beautiful, white-breasted blackbirds. Never seen anything like them."

Daphne's chin jutted back in surprise. She hadn't expected the birds to actually be inside the cave. She glanced over at Roger, who gave her another mysterious wink.

"Sharon?" Roger asked. "Ready?"

Daphne's mother followed Roger into the dark cave. While they waited, she turned to study her father, who was scrolling through the digital images he'd captured on the back of his camera. He'd recently buzzed his hair again. Even though he had retired from the army years ago, he always buzzed his gray hair in the summertime, and if it weren't for the pot belly hanging over his belt and the worry lines around his eyes and forehead, he'd still look like a jarhead.

He took a few sideways steps closer to her and said, "Take a look at this one. You can see them really good."

Two birds nested in a shelf of rock. One looked directly at the camera.

"I thought Roger said no pics," Daphne said.

"I turned off the flash. I didn't think the birds would show up, but the dim light of the flashlight worked."

Daphne nodded.

Unexpectedly, her father put an arm around her shoulders. "How's my little girl doing?"

Little girl? Her stomach clenched, and she wanted to burst into tears. He hadn't called her his little girl in forever. "Okay." She suddenly felt like burying her face in his chest, but she fought the urge.

"I'm glad you talked us into staying. This has been fun today."

Before Daphne could reply, Sharon and Roger emerged from the cave, Sharon smiling from ear to ear.

When they were a safe distance from the opening, Sharon said, "They really are pretty."

Daphne was beginning to suspect with growing disappointment that there was no game today when she noticed a dozen or more bugs crawling from her mother's shorts' pocket. They were brownish gray, about an inch in length, with at least ten tiny feet. They had two long antennae and backs that looked like armor. They made her think of tiny armadillos, but with pinchers trailing behind. Sharon seemed oblivious to them until they reached her pale pink blouse.

Sharon flinched back and screamed, swatting the bugs as she jumped from one foot to the other. "Get 'em off! Get 'em off!"

Joe tried to help her, but Sharon ran around, flailing her arms. "Oh, God! Get 'em off!"

"Hold still and let me help you," Joe said, exasperated.

Roger said, "They aren't harmful. Calm down. Don't scare the birds."

"Get 'em off me, Joe!"

Daphne's dad swatted the bugs to the ground, but a few landed on Sharon's bare legs, making her scream and kick in a frenzied dance. She made Daphne think of a circus clown.

"What are they?" Daphne asked, trying not to smile, as she helped her father scrape them away from her mother's jerking body.

"Rock lice," Roger said. "They aren't poisonous, and their bites don't sting."

"They bite?" Sharon squealed. Her entire body flailed about. She scratched at her scalp and twitched her mouth as she clamped her eyes closed.

"Almost got 'em all," Joe said. "There."

Sharon couldn't hold still. "Are you sure? All of 'em?" She untucked her blouse and shook it.

Daphne and Joe looked all over Sharon but saw no more of the rock lice.

"You're good, Mama," Daphne said.

Sharon stopped flailing and gazed at Daphne, her jaw hanging open.

Daphne felt the blood rush once again to her face. "What?"

Tears pooled in Sharon's eyes and spilled down her cheeks. At first, Daphne thought her mother was crying with relief, to have all the bugs off her body. But then her mother said, "You haven't called me 'Mama' in two years. Did you know that?"

Daphne *did* know that. Since Kara's death, since her mother had said those haunting words ("You mean you heard and did nothing?"), Daphne hadn't been able to call her mother the name she had called her all her life. The horrible guilt she had felt, the guilt she had seen reflected back at her in her mother's eyes, had made her pull away and erect walls, and from that moment on it had been "Mother" and sometimes "Mom." She hadn't meant to call her "Mama" just then, either, but her guard had come down, and the old name had slipped out.

Joe hugged Sharon and patted Daphne on the back. "It's been an exciting day," he said.

Daphne avoided her parents' eyes, holding back tears. She cleared her throat and asked, "Where do we go from here, Roger?"

"Don't you wanna take a look?" Roger asked.

Everyone turned their eyes on Daphne, waiting for her reply.

"Do you think I'll regret it if I don't?" Daphne asked Roger, speaking in a kind of code.

"I think so," he said. "Come on. I'll be right there with you."

Daphne felt her knees about to buckle as she followed Roger through the narrow opening into the cave. She fought off images of getting trapped, of the cave collapsing on top of them and crushing them. He shined the flashlight on his face, holding one finger to his lips. Then he pointed his finger and moved the light toward a nest. He didn't shine the light directly on the birds; rather, he pointed the light to the right of them and allowed the outer rim to cast a soft glow across the nesting pair, so as not to startle them.

Then Roger moved the light to their left. Daphne searched for another nest, but instead, was startled to see a black hooded figure. She flinched, but Roger held her hand and stilled her. A black-gloved hand lifted the hood, and the light shone on Cam.

Daphne gasped.

Cam moved a finger to his lips in the same way Roger had, warning her to stay silent. Then he reached into a pail with a long set of tongs, plucked up a rock louse, and slowly reached over to the nest. Roger followed Cam's arm with the flashlight as Cam released the bug a few inches from the birds. Daphne watched in amazement as one of the birds snatched the bug up in its beak and shared it with its mate. Then Roger took her hand and led her from the cave. She turned back to look at Cam but could no longer see him in the darkness.

Daphne wondered as they followed the trail back to the jeep if Cam or Roger had put the handful of lice in her mother's pocket. She smiled at Roger several times as they ascended the hill, unable to contain how pleased she was with the game. It took all her self-control to hide her eagerness for the next one.

Back in her room, as she freshened up before lunch, she thought about her mother's reaction to being called, "Mama." Tears threatened to well in her eyes when she realized the added pain that she'd caused her mother these past two years. Daphne hadn't done it to hurt her mom; she'd done it to protect herself. Avoiding terms of endearment like "Mama" and "Daddy" was one of many ways she had prepared herself to leave everyone behind. Even though she was still upset over what they had put her through here on the island, she realized today that she'd never, ever stopped loving them. In a strange way, being punished by them through this therapy and having the opportunity to punish them back worked to bring them closer together.

After calling Brock and learning he wasn't hungry, Daphne walked with her parents to the banquet hall for lunch where they sat at a table with Cam and Bridget. She felt members of both the older crowd at Hortense's table and the younger crowd at another looking at her with conspiratorial smiles. Did they all know what had transpired on the bird trail? She smiled back at them and enjoyed her lunch. At their table, her father retold what had happened with the bugs, and even her mother laughed.

Daphne turned the silver bracelet around and around her left wrist, pushed herself to be brave, and said, "That's Mama for you."

Her mother and father beamed.

Then Cam said, "We're taking a sunset cruise this evening after dinner." He winked at Daphne. "I hope you can all go. It's beautiful, isn't it Daph?"

It was Daphne's turn to beam as she wondered which among Brock and her parents would be manipulated into jumping into the sea.

"Absolutely," she said. "You'll love it."

CHAPTER FOUR

Snakes

After lunch, Daphne said goodbye to her parents in front of their unit before continuing down the path to Brock's. Cam and Bridget caught up with her and pulled her aside by the tennis courts, which were abandoned.

"Want to have some fun with Brock today?" Bridget couldn't stop giggling.

Daphne glanced at Cam. "What do you have in mind?"

Cam gave her a mischievous smile. "Let's just say today would be a great day for a picnic."

"I just ate," Daphne said.

"But Brock hasn't," Bridget pointed out. "You could make him a couple of sandwiches in the room and suggest eating on the bluff over-looking the beach."

"Anyway, there are extra blankets in the chest at the foot of his bed," Cam said. "Use one of those for the picnic, and don't be surprised if a few snakes join you on the bluff."

"What?" The corners of Daphne's mouth reached all the way to her cheeks. This sounded like fun. "Not poisonous ones."

"Of course not," Cam said. "Perfectly harmless, but scary as hell."

"You have to pretend to be frightened of them, too," Bridget coached her. "And don't look like you're waiting for something to happen."

"We almost didn't tell you for that very reason," Cam said.

Bridget put her hands on her slim hips. "You could ruin the whole exercise if you don't play it cool."

"Just spread the blanket next to the big boulder on top of the bluff," Cam said. "We'll be hiding on the other side with the snakes. Go in about an hour, so we have time to set everything up."

"What should I do when we see the snakes?" Daphne asked. "Run?"

"Improvise," Cam said. "You can't really mess this up, unless you're obviously expecting something to happen."

"You know the one rule, right?" Bridget said with a sober look on her face.

"Right."

"And remember," Cam said. "It's not why, but what."

Cam and Bridget walked off hand in hand, leaving Daphne to process this new information. With a smile on her lips, she turned and headed for Brock's unit.

When he came to the door, he had that oh-so-hot, fresh-from-a-nap look about him. She wanted to throw her arms around him and push him onto the bed. She almost forgot all about the picnic with the snakes. Almost.

"I didn't sleep well last night," he said. "The prank with the ghosts freaked me out."

She didn't want to admit as he closed the door behind her and took her in his arms that she had had the best night of sleep since her arrival. The exercise with the ghosts had purged her of anger and guilt and a whole lot of messed up feelings.

"I'm tired from the morning hike with my parents. Mind if I join you?"

He grinned in that sexy way that almost made her forget she was mad at him. "Do you have to ask?"

She kicked off her shoes and curled beside him on the bed, offering to scratch his back. He purred like a kitten beneath her fingernails. She had to suck in her lips to keep from giggling. She couldn't wait to see him scream.

"Reminds me of the good ol' days," he said softly.

Her heart skipped a beat as the smile left her. How could she be so cruel?

"Remember that time I got snowed in at your house?" he asked.

"Of course I do." Her parents had let him stay overnight on their sleeper-sofa.

"I prayed for hours that you'd come visit me in the middle of the night. I was shocked when you actually appeared. I thought I was dreaming."

"It *felt* like a dream." She sighed. Those were the days when she was still trying to cheer him up after his mother had died—before Daphne had begun to feel guilty about her own happiness. It wasn't long after that snow day that Daphne started folding like a dying rose further and further into herself as she erected thorns.

Brock turned over on his back and pulled her in for a kiss. His lips were trembling beneath hers, and when she opened her eyes, she saw him gazing at her with tears in his eyes.

"Brock?"

"If only you knew how much I've missed you." His voice cracked. "I thought I wasn't ever going to get you back."

She wrapped her arms around his waist and laid her cheek against his chest, unable to meet his eyes. Here he was confessing his unending love for her, and what was she doing? She was planning to scare the living daylights out of him.

Brock slipped his hand beneath her t-shirt and returned the back-scratch. His nails softly caressed her skin, making her aware of how tense she had been as she relaxed the muscles in her shoulders and neck. Taking in a deep breath, she relaxed into his chest and closed her eyes. A sigh escaped her lips. Maybe she wouldn't suggest the picnic after all. This felt so entirely wonderful, and she hadn't realized how tired she was. A nap in Brock's arms as he gently scratched her back sounded heavenly.

"Mmm," she purred. "Don't stop."

Sometime later, her body twitched and woke her up. Had she really fallen asleep?

"You okay?" Brock murmured in a sleepy voice.

"Yeah." She glanced at the clock on the nightstand. She'd been asleep for twenty minutes. "You hungry?"

He lifted his arms above his head and stretched the length of his body. She watched the muscles on his arms and chest with fascination. He made a sexy, stretching sound in his throat, bringing a smile to her face. She still wasn't sure what to do about the picnic.

Then she realized her scarf was off-center, exposing part of her bald head. She jumped from the bed and went to the bathroom mirror to fix it.

"What's wrong?" Brock called.

"Nothing," she lied. "Why don't we go have a picnic?"

On their way to the bluff, they ran into Daphne's parents sunbathing on loungers by the pool. Her mother had a book in her hand and her father was watching the gulls soaring overhead.

"Hey, you two," her father said when they approached. "Where are you off to?"

"We're going for a picnic," Daphne said.

"Sounds fun, honey," her mother said with a smile. "This turned out to be a nice retreat after all, didn't it?"

Daphne couldn't prevent the grin from crossing her face. "It sure did."

"Have fun, sweetheart," her father said. "We'll catch ya later."

With the blanket draped over one shoulder, Brock led Daphne up the wooden steps to the boardwalk, but instead of descending the steps to the beach, they took the bridge to the bluff. She noticed another couple picnicking in the opposite direction—on the hill of yellow poppies on the other end of the bridge. She didn't recognize them, though.

Brock started to spread the blanket on a flat spot.

"Over here," she said, pointing near the large boulder. Her heart was racing, and she hoped Brock couldn't see her fingers twitching with excitement.

"The view is better from over here," Brock said.

"But I want to lean on this rock," she said. "I'm still worn out from all I've been put through on this island."

The guilt card was well-played, and Brock yielded to her will. She smiled as she unloaded the snacks and sodas in her arms and helped him smooth out the blanket. Then they made themselves comfortable. She leaned her back against the boulder, trying to hide her nervous excitement. He lay with his head in her lap and started on his sandwiches. Her Diet Coke can fizzled to life when she popped the tab. The sound made her jump.

"What?" he asked, looking up at her.

She leaned over and pecked his lips with her own. "I'm just excited to be here with you."

They talked of trivial things for a while as they gazed out to sea, Daphne wondering the whole time when the snakes would appear. Brock finished both sandwiches. Her soda can was nearly empty.

"There's a sunset cruise this evening," she said. "My parents and I are going. Come with?"

"I wouldn't miss it," he said.

She searched her mind for more small talk, wishing Cam would just get on with it.

"Did you know that Stan and Bridget and even Cam jump into the sea from up here?" she asked, hoping to hint to her friends to hurry up and do something.

"You've done it, too. That was my grisly introduction to this place: the love of my life diving from the highest rock into the crashing waves below. My heart nearly stopped beating."

The love of his life.

Tears brimmed in her eyes. "I only did it because I was scared out of my mind."

"I know that, now," he said. "But at the time, Dr. Gray hadn't yet explained everything to me."

"What did she say to you, anyway?" Now she was curious.

"She told me that sometimes it takes something really dramatic and painful to help you let go of your mistakes and move on with your life."

Cam had once told her the same thing. "What else did she say?"

"She said it's not why, but what."

"What do you think that means, anyway?"

"She said we shouldn't get hung up on why this or that happens or why we do this or that. We should instead focus on what we choose to do with our lives."

"Do you agree with her?" Daphne uncrossed and re-crossed her legs.

"I think so. I mean, I'm not sure that there's really a single meaning or purpose that's our destiny. I think we have to make our own meaning."

"So, what else did she say?"

Brock stiffened. She could feel him against her legs. Had Dr. Gray said something upsetting to him?

"What's wrong?" she asked.

"Don't move," he whispered.

Adrenaline surged through her as she realized the moment had come. Without moving her head, she glanced as far as her eyes could reach and that's when she saw them: Two thick black snakes coiled around Brock's foot.

"Oh, crap," she said. "What do we do?"

"Don't move. Just hold still." He spoke quickly, like he was on the edge of panic as the two snakes slithered up his leg.

"Do you know if they're poisonous?"

"No. Oh, God."

The snakes had reached his thigh.

"We've got to do something, Brock. What if they bite?"

"Grab them behind the head."

"Are you kidding me?"

"Grab them behind the head and fling them away. Do you think you can do that?"

"What if they bite me? I'm scared, Brock." She was enjoying his fear a bit too much, she thought. She felt like a participant in one of those set-up reality shows, like *Fear Factor* and *The Jamie Kennedy Experiment.*

He sat up, and, in one quick move, he reached with both hands and grabbed the snakes as he jumped to his feet. Then he flung the poor creatures out to sea.

Daphne climbed to her feet, her heart going wild in her chest. What a rush!

"God, Brock! You were amazing! I can't believe you just threw them off of you like that!" Especially when, unlike she, he didn't know they weren't deadly.

He took her in his arms. "Are you okay?"

She nodded as he caressed her cheek and consoled her. Consoled *her.* She felt a little bad about that, but not *that* bad. It had been thrilling. "Are you?"

He nodded. "Let's get out of here.

She glanced at the boulder as they packed up their things but saw no sign of her fellow conspirators.

As they gathered up the blanket and strolled across the wooden bridge toward the resort, Daphne gazed out at the far-reaching sea, soaked in its brilliance, and smiled. She felt lighter, happier, and more excited than she had ever felt in the two years since Kara's death.

CHAPTER FIVE

Shark Attack

Later that evening after dinner, Roger and Vince shuttled those taking the sunset cruise out to Willows Anchorage to the resort's private pier. Daphne and her parents rode with Roger, who then returned for Brock, Cam, and Bridget. Vince drove another jeep with Emma, Gregory, and the older woman, Mary Ellen—the woman who'd reminded Daphne of a Mrs. Santa Claus. Vince parked the jeep at Willows Anchorage and joined the cruise, but Roger returned to the resort. The captain welcomed everyone aboard and introductions were made. After life vests were distributed to those who wanted one—namely, Mary Ellen and Vince—the boat departed from the pier as the passengers lined up along the railing and gazed out to sea.

The sun was a large dark-orange globe nestled in thinly stretched pink clouds. The sea, relatively calm, reflected stripes in a color somewhere in between. Gulls flew low overhead, as though expecting to be fed. Other boats sailed farther out in the distance, but not close enough for Daphne and her group to see their passengers. Although the wind blew more swiftly here on the water, it wasn't the all-out accost Daphne had experienced on the ride from the mainland.

Daphne was giddy. The bit of guilt she had felt over the earlier exercise with the snakes had vanished, and in its place was the thrill of anticipation. She never did learn who had pretended to be the sharks during the supposed attack on her a week ago, but after what Pete had told her of his faked death using Stan's deep-sea diving gear, she suspected Stan and Pete were two of the three. The fact that Dave was almost always with Vince, and wasn't today, led her to believe he would be playing a third shark.

As the boat rounded the harbor, Cam leaned close to Daphne's ear and whispered, "The headlamp on the captain's cap is really a livestream camera. Take a look."

Captain Jim wore a baseball cap with what looked like a headlamp attached to the bill. He'd worn the same thing the day Daphne had taken her cruise. She gaped as she realized her shark attack had been broadcasted. Why and to whom? Was Prospero watching from inside her office? Her memory of what Larry had once said about the watchers made her crinkle her forehead in wonder. *Were* there others watching the exercises? Dr. Reynolds, maybe? Arturo Gomez?

Brock, who stood on the other side of her, leaned in and murmured, "What was that about?"

She planted a quick kiss on his lips. "Nothing. He just said something funny about the captain."

"What?"

Daphne's mind reeled as she nervously turned the silver bracelet on her wrist. "Um, that he looks like he has a wooden leg." Daphne inwardly groaned and scolded herself for not thinking fast on her feet. She'd have to do better if she was going to be any help with the therapeutic games.

Brock glanced over at Jim. "Come on, what did Cam really say?"

Daphne squared herself to Brock. "Ssh. You have to swear not to tell."

He nodded. "I swear."

"Cam likes Bridget, but don't let on you know." Daphne felt a little good and a little bad about the lie. Hadn't *Brock* lied to *her*? Besides, she had a feeling Cam *did* like Bridget.

Brock grinned and turned back to the sea, apparently satisfied.

Just then, Gregory pointed out at least a half dozen sea lions sunning on a rock near the edge of the harbor. Jim turned the boat toward them. Daphne's dad took photos as they stopped and idled twenty yards from the sea lions, until Bridget lifted her sundress over her head and dived into the sea.

Like last time, Cam slapped his thighs and said, "I can't believe she's actually doing it!"

"Are you sure that's safe?" Mary Ellen asked.

"Absolutely," Jim said.

Cam turned to Daphne and, with his eyes, motioned toward the water.

What? She lifted her brows at him.

He held a finger discreetly near his chest and pointed toward the water. His lips mouthed, "Jump in."

Cam said, "It's pretty safe, Mary Ellen. Just ask Daphne. She went swimming with Bridget the last time we took the cruise and had a close encounter with the sea lions, isn't that right, Daph?"

He wanted her to go in again? Why should she go in? Shouldn't Brock be encouraged to swim after Bridget? That seemed the most logical thing to her. Daphne narrowed her eyes with uncertainty. What if her scarf came off?

Daphne looked from one face to another, all eyes on her. "Right. It was...awesome." Was she really meant to jump in again?

Mary Ellen said, "Oh, I'd love to see that, dear. If I were younger, I'd go, too."

"If you're sure it's safe, I'd like to get a picture," Joe added.

Both Cam and Mary Ellen were silently urging Daphne to jump. As she glanced over at Emma, Gregory, and Vince, she could feel all of them willing her to dive into the sea. She wasn't about to remove her shorts and t-shirt and strip to her underwear in front of her parents, so she jumped in, clothes and all, careful to keep her head above water so her scarf stayed secure, and swam out past Bridget toward the sea lions, all the while wondering why it was she who was being forced to play the victim again.

The water was cold and exhilarating but added to her trembling. Even though she knew the sharks that were coming for her weren't real, she was nevertheless nervous about how the game would go down. Then Daphne had her Aha moment: Hortense wanted Daphne in the water with the sharks because losing Daphne was her parents and Brock's greatest fear.

She used to fantasize about how her parents might react if she were dying. That night she had taken the bottles of Prozac and Tylenol, she had fantasized about what her parents would say over her dead body— how they would hold her and kiss her and say lovely things to her. They would feel terrible for anything bad they had ever said to her. They would finally love her as much as they had loved Kara.

She blinked a few tears from her eyes and glanced back at the boat just as Bridget was being helped back onto the deck by Cam and Gregory. Daphne eased out toward the sea lions, taking the opportunity to get another good look at them. They really were amazing creatures—golden in color with dog-like faces, little flaps for ears, and long whiskers.

"Hello," she said to one of them, who had turned to study her.

Then the screams began.

Daphne pretended not to see the three dorsal fins approaching from her left. She waved at the boat, offering a repeat of her thumbs up. She saw her mother leaning over the rail, with one hand at her mouth and another pointing.

Before Daphne could catch her breath, she was suddenly dragged beneath the surface. She reached for her scarf as the water swept it from her head, and she kicked and pulled, but a hand caught her wrist. It was Stan behind a diver's mask. He fit the mouthpiece from his oxygen to her mouth. She gagged at first, needing to force water out. She scrambled to the surface, coughing and gagging. The screams from the boat startled her. She took a breath and went under, anxious to conceal her bald head. Then, after emptying the air in her lungs, she returned the mouthpiece to her lips and sucked in, relaxing her limbs in the water. Stan held one hand on her shoulder to prevent her from floating to the surface and, with the other, gave her the same thumbs up she had just given the passengers on the boat. He said something, but she couldn't make out his words as the bubbles floated from his lips. Then Pete came up beside her with a knife, and Dave came up behind, and before she knew what was happening, Pete cut a gash into her calf just below her knee.

It stung and the salt water burned. She kicked and pushed away from them, angry and shocked that they would physically harm her for the sake of the exercise, but she found no resistance as the men quickly swam, with flippers on their feet and oxygen on their backs (beneath plastic dorsal fins), down deep and out of sight.

When Daphne emerged, coughing and choking, and without her scarf, which she'd lost in the chaos, she saw what had scattered the sharks. Brock and her father had jumped in. Both men swam toward her, her father floundering and getting nowhere, Brock reaching her in a matter of minutes. The life buoy landed a few feet away.

"What are you doing?" Daphne asked over the shouts from the boat.

"Just grab on to this buoy and don't let go."

"What about my dad?" Blood pooled around them, and now she was afraid she'd attract real sharks.

The boat dragged her and Brock away from where the dorsal fins had reappeared near the sea lions. Daphne craned her neck to look at her father barely holding his head above water.

"Something's wrong," she said.

She let go of the buoy, which was towing them in the opposite direction of her father, to swim to his aid. Brock grabbed her before she'd gotten very far.

"Take the buoy. I'll get your father."

Brock kept his eyes on the sharks, which were moving in from ten yards away.

"But…"

"Dammit, Daphne. I'm faster than you are." His brows were bent, his eyes fixed on her father.

She scrambled for the buoy and watched Brock swim freestyle toward her dad as the boat towed her to safety. Once she was on deck, the boat headed for Brock, who swam sidestroke with an arm around her father's chest. Gregory dropped the buoy over and they all helped Joe aboard.

It wasn't until both Brock and her father were on the deck and a towel had been pressed against the bleeding gash in her leg that Daphne noticed her mother. She was retching over the opposite side of the boat. As Daphne went to her, Sharon wiped her mouth with the back of an arm and fell to her knees in a heap, clinging to the rail. She was whiter than a ghost and trembling, teeth chattering, tears streaming down her cheeks. Daphne knelt next to her.

"We're okay," Daphne said. "No one's hurt, Mama."

Sharon nodded and didn't speak, apparently unable to. She reached a quivering hand out to touch Daphne's cheek.

Daphne held her mother's clammy hand to her cheek and gave her a faint smile, feeling horrible about what she'd just put her through. Before she could say another word, her mother leaned over the side of the boat, which slowly headed for the pier, and was sick again.

Daphne, flooded with guilt, rubbed her mother's back with one hand as she pressed the towel against her wound with the other. This wasn't right. How had she ever justified tormenting the people she loved most? She glanced around at the others, who were watching her closely, as though they suspected what she was thinking.

"How's your leg?" Jim asked.

Sharon's eyes widened. "What happened to your leg, Honey? Let me see."

Daphne lifted the towel. A two-inch gash, not very deep, was just below her knee on the back side of her calf. Blood and water mixed together and dripped down her skin. She returned the towel and said, "It's nothing. It wasn't even…"

"Looks like a pectoral got ya," Jim said.

"A what?" Daphne asked.

"The shark finned you," Jim said. "We're lucky he didn't bite."

Sharon Janus fell on her bottom, looking woozy.

"Mama! Don't listen to him! It was…"

"Doesn't look too bad," Cam interrupted. "Let me help you put pressure on it." Cam moved up beside her and held the towel firmly against her leg. He shook his head, willing her to keep her mouth shut, but Daphne turned from him to her mother's frail form, like a wet sock, beside her. Cam grabbed her arms and added, "And here, take my hat so your head doesn't burn."

Her mother put her face in her hands and wept. "Why did we ever send you to this place!"

Daphne fitted the cap with a shaky hand. Her pulse was off the charts as she licked her lips and said, "Mama, it's okay. This wasn't real; it was just..."

The boat suddenly swerved to the right, causing people to lose their balance and tumble to the deck with shrieks of surprise.

Cam moved even closer to Daphne and whispered at her ear, "Don't do it. You'll ruin everything." His eyes were urgent, almost fearful.

"My apologies!" the captain shouted. "Everyone okay? Joe?"

Daphne glanced across the deck for her father and saw him lying on his back on a bench clutching his chest.

"Oh my God!" she cried, hurrying to his side where Brock bent over him. "Is he okay?"

"He's having chest pains," Brock replied. "I think they started in the water."

Daphne crouched beside her father, putting a hand on his chest. "Daddy? You alright?"

"I'll be fine," he said, not getting up. "Just give me a minute to catch my breath."

Daphne could no longer stand what she'd done.

Soon her mother was there, too. "Joe? What's wrong?"

"We need to get him to a doctor!" Daphne said.

"*I'm* a doctor," Mary Ellen said, joining Daphne and her mother at Joe's side. "Jim, take us back to the resort." She turned to Daphne's mother. "Don't worry, dear. He'll be safe in my care."

Daphne narrowed her eyes at the old woman. Was she really a doctor, or was she pretending? Why hadn't Cam introduced her as a doctor? He had, after all, introduced Hortense's colleague in behavioral psychology as Dr. Lee Reynolds. It seemed odd that, if Mary Ellen were also a doctor, that the title was never mentioned.

She watched on as Mary Ellen asked her father a series of questions, which the woman might have learned from a number of medical dramas on television.

Vince drove Daphne and her parents directly from the pier down to the main building. Mary Ellen and the others waited for Roger, whom Vince passed on the way down. Daphne escorted her parents to the second floor to the supposed infirmary, anxious to find evidence that it really was an infirmary. When she saw all the familiar paraphernalia—a reception desk and waiting area, an examination room with anatomical posters, a narrow table covered in paper, a desk with a rolling stool, tongue depressors, cotton balls, a scale, and even an ear checker, Daphne had to admit that if it were a suite full of props, it was convincing. She still wasn't sure if she believed Mary Ellen was a doctor, but she did think someone there must be one, and it only made sense that an operation of this magnitude would have a resident physician and an infirmary.

Mary Ellen soon arrived with Brock and Cam trailing her. After an initial exam, she sent an assistant for an EKG machine and asked everyone but Joe to wait outside. The others went to shower and change, but Daphne and her mother sat in two chairs just outside of the examining room. Mary Ellen had cleaned and bandaged Daphne's leg on the ride in, using the boat's first aid kit. When they had arrived at the infirmary, she was given a bottle of antibiotics to prevent infection. Daphne had a towel wrapped around her, and she still had Cam's cap on her head, but her clothes were still wet, and she trembled. Her mother had begged her to return to her room for a hot shower and change of clothes, promising an update as soon as she knew anything, but Daphne was afraid to leave her parents.

"Go back to your room," her mother said again. "We'll call as soon as we're done here."

Daphne had a better idea. She stood up, gave her mother a weak smile, and marched down the hallway toward room 200.

Daphne knocked on Hortense Gray's office door but did not wait for a response before opening it. She was shocked to see Arturo Gomez holding the doctor in his arms. They separated, the resort owner greeted Daphne, and then he excused himself as he hastened from the room.

"What can I do for you?" Hortense asked unapologetically as she stood behind her desk. "Please, have a seat."

Daphne remained standing, confused. Wasn't Dr. Reynolds supposed to be in love with Hortense Gray? So Mr. Gomez was as well? "Is Mary Ellen really a doctor?"

Dr. Gray sighed. "No, but Philip Johnson is, and he's pretending to be her nurse, so you can rest assured your father is getting proper care."

"I don't want to continue."

"What?"

"I'm afraid for my mom and dad's health. The shark attack was way too hard on them."

Hortense smiled. "You don't give them enough credit. From what I see on my screen, your father's EKG is normal."

"What screen?"

"I told you," Hortense sat on her high-back chair. "I am aware of everything that happens on this island. I have eyes and ears everywhere."

"Live-stream cameras?"

"That's right. Perhaps I'll show you."

"Now?"

"Not now. Soon."

Tears of relief over her father's normal EKG spilled from Daphne's eyes. She wanted to sit down, but she didn't want to get the green chenille chair wet.

Hortense interrupted Daphne's thoughts. "I just received an email indicating that your father's chest pains and palpitations were likely caused by a panic attack. There's no evidence of heart trouble. He's been given a mild sedative and told to take it easy tomorrow."

"So, no more games."

"We'll give him tomorrow off, but he'll be fine after that." Hortense crossed her arms. "Can you not appreciate the incredible progress the three of you have already made in your relationship? The therapy is working. There's no reason to abort. Your father's panic attacks are manageable, and his heart is fine. We'll move on as planned."

Daphne bit on her lower lip. The doctor spoke the truth. Progress had been made. Maybe Daphne should do as Cam had said and trust Hortense.

"Do you have any other questions or concerns, Daphne?"

She shook her head. "No, ma'am. Thank you." With that, Daphne left the room.

Back in her cabana, after a warm shower and a quick visit from her parents and Brock, Daphne snuggled under the covers, in her pj's, with her poetry journal, reflecting on the day. She had to admit that she and her parents had not interacted like they had today since before Kara's death. She closed her eyes and allowed herself to think about those days, when they were a happy family. She missed Kara and Joey so much. She had missed her parents, too, but for the first time in two years, she felt like she was with them again—not just living in the same location, but together, *really* together in spirit.

She wrote:

This time when I reach for you,
I know that you are there.
I feel you smiling down on me,
I feel you everywhere.

She was about to drift off when she heard a soft rap at her door. She pulled the hoodie over her head, climbed from the covers, and peered through the window. It was Brock.

"Hey," she said, opening the door.

"Hey. I couldn't sleep. Can I stay here tonight?" He smelled clean in his t-shirt and basketball shorts, his hair neatly combed.

She gave him a radiant smile and said, "I'd like that."

C H A P T E R   S I X

Caught on Tape

The sun slanted through the front windows, creating two bright lines across the bed and Brock's back. Daphne lifted her hand and reached toward the stripes of sunshine, making shadows on the comforter. Her legs were warm up against Brock, her toes tucked beneath his shin. He was lightly snoring on his stomach, his arms bent over his pillow above his head, his face turned toward her. She studied the tanned bicep, visible beneath the short-sleeved t-shirt. Then she looked at his dark lashes lying softly against his cheeks, his thin nose and his open, thick lips.

God, she loved him.

His lids fluttered open, and his eyes met hers, which she widened with surprise before she pulled the covers over her head—her bald head. She had removed the hoodie during the night and had slept in a tank top. Why oh why hadn't she put it back on as soon as she had awakened?

"What are you doing?" he asked, his voice hoarse and low.

"Don't look at me."

"Don't be ridiculous."

"I'm not."

"You do realize you're still beautiful, don't you?"

She didn't reply.

"Look at me," he insisted.

She remained hidden.

He wrestled for the covers, and she resisted, fighting him.

"Stop!" she said. "I mean it."

"Look at me, Daph." He continued to wrestle with her. He straddled her and used both hands to wrench the covers out of her grip. "Will you stop? I love you. And you're beautiful. There's no reason to hide from me."

She covered her face and cried. The morning had started off so nicely, and now she lay beneath Brock, mortified. "Get off!"

"Look at me. Stop this nonsense. You're making me mad."

"You're making *me* mad! Get off!"

He kissed the backs of her fingers. Then he took her face in his hands and kissed, softly, gently, the very top of her head, over and over, every inch of it, while she lay beneath him sobbing. He was tender, and she was grateful—grateful that he hadn't easily given in to her tantrum and rolled away. She had wanted him to fight for her, to show he meant what he had said when he had said she was beautiful. She hadn't believed he could stomach her bald head, and now he was kissing it, was making love to it.

God, she loved this guy.

A moment later, he pried her fingers from her face and kissed her eyelids, her wet cheeks, and her mouth.

"Let me love you," he whispered with his mouth against hers. "Please. It's all I've ever wanted." He kissed her softly—her forehead, her nose, her eyes, her cheeks. "I was so scared of losing you yesterday. You can't imagine how terrified. Those bastard sharks. I wanted to kill them."

She felt warm tears drop from his face onto hers. She opened her eyes and reached her arms around his neck, pulling him close, ready to finally let him love her.

After they had each showered and dressed—she in another borrowed hoodie now that her scarf was ruined—they met her parents for breakfast. As soon as they arrived, her parents hugged her and asked about the cut on her leg. Daphne told them it was fine, and, as they filled their plates in the buffet line, she listened to them replay the events of the day before—how terrifying it had been to see those sharks, and the blood, and her father floundering, and how grateful they were that their baby girl was alright. Daphne lost her appetite. The guilt was getting to her.

Hortense and Lee Reynolds and their ilk were sitting at their usual table, pretending not to watch her and her family make their way to theirs. The younger crowd of regulars hadn't yet arrived, except for Dave and Vince. When she glanced their way, Dave winked and smiled before saying something to Vince. Vince grinned, nodded, and gave Daphne a finger wave. As the hour passed, the others trickled in: Emma and Gregory entered holding hands, followed a few minutes later by Stan. Cam and Bridget were the last of the group to arrive. They came together, each with glowing faces, tan from the sun, but beaming with happiness, too. This made Daphne wonder again if there was something more than friendship between them.

"I'm real impressed with the food here," Daphne's father said as he loaded his fork with a bite of waffle and scrambled egg.

"And the rooms are nice," Sharon added.

Daphne stifled a laugh and thought, *Well at least there's that. You're about to be tortured out of your mind, but at least you'll be able to say the food was good and the rooms were nice.*

"You okay, Daph?" Brock asked.

"What? Oh, yeah. Fine."

"Did you remember to take your antibiotic this morning?" her mother asked.

She hadn't. "I'll take it as soon as I get back."

"You won't want an infection in that wound," her dad said.

She suppressed the urge to say, "Obviously."

She didn't have to fight hard to keep from speaking her thoughts, though, because at that moment, a scene broke out across the room at the younger crowd's table. Hortense Gray stood, stiff and frowning, in front of her son and Emma. The table was quiet and still, except for Gregory, who looked up at his mother with eyes of resentment.

"Come with me, Gregory," Dr. Gray commanded.

Daphne expected Greg to put up a fight, but he hung his head and left the table. He followed his mother from the dining hall. Once they had gone, a murmur erupted around the younger crowd's table, and Emma was in tears.

"I wonder what that was about," Sharon said.

Daphne shrugged and acted like it had been nothing, but she, too, was curious. Was Hortense Gray upset over her son's relationship with Emma? Maybe she didn't want him mingling with the natives, so to speak—the natives being the patients. That seemed a bit ironic to Daphne, since she had walked in on the doctor and her former patient, Arturo Gomez, the previous evening.

As Daphne, Brock, and her parents were carrying their trays of empty plates back to the bussing shelves, Dr. Gray returned to the dining hall. Greg wasn't with her, and she wore the expression of a conqueror. Before returning to her table, Dr. Gray walked up to Daphne and her parents—Brock had just gone to the restroom.

"We have something special planned tomorrow evening. It's the highlight of the summer," the doctor said smiling. "Our costume ball."

"But we didn't bring costumes," Sharon said.

"Oh, that's no problem." Dr. Gray flapped her hand in a dismissive gesture. "We have an entire roomful for you to peruse. I happen to be a costume aficionado and have amassed quite a collection over the years."

"Interesting," Joe said. "Does *everybody* dress up?"

"Absolutely," Dr. Gray replied. "It's required."

Joe wrinkled his nose at Sharon and then Daphne.

Dr. Gray added, "And it's an important part of the therapy."

"Well, in that case," Sharon didn't finish her sentence.

"I'll have Cameron show you my collection." With that, Dr. Gray excused herself and returned to her table where the older crowd still sat, as though waiting, like students, to be dismissed from class.

"Don't be a party pooper," Sharon warned Joe before Daphne's father could complain.

They chatted together as they made their way to the elevator, where Daphne forced herself to ride. Her father asked Brock if he knew about any fishing on the island, and her mother asked about the spa, and then they reached the ground level and exited the building. Once they neared the pool, Daphne and Brock parted ways with her parents, who wanted to lounge around a bit. Then Brock put an arm around her as they strolled toward her room.

"Aren't you hot in the hoodie?" he asked her.

"I think I'll check the gift shop. Something tells me they carry a lot of scarves."

Cam caught up with them from behind and took Daphne by the elbow.

"Hold on," he said. "Dr. Gray wants to show you something."

Daphne glanced at Brock. "Both of us?"

"You go on without me," Brock said. "I want to go for a swim."

"Meet you later?" she asked him.

Brock kissed the side of her head. "Absolutely."

Cam linked arms with her and took her back toward the main building, while Brock headed for the cabanas.

"How sure are you about him?" Cam asked.

"What do you mean?"

"I mean, are you sure he's the one for you?"

She cracked a smile and playfully rammed her shoulder against his. "Jealous?"

"Hell, yeah." He was smiling, too.

"What about Bridget? Aren't you two a thing?"

"I guess so." He opened the door of the main building for her to enter first. "I like her alright. I like her a lot, actually. But you'll always be my number one."

Heat rushed to her face, and she was glad he was behind her so he couldn't see it. She tried to brush it off. "Yeah right."

"Seriously."

"You're crazy. We're best friends, right?"

"Always," he said with a half-smile that filled her with guilt.

They took the stairs up to Dr. Gray's office and knocked on the door.

"Enter!" the doctor's voice called out in her usual stiff and formal manner.

Cam opened the door to the chaotic room, which had a few more art pieces stacked on the floor right by the entryway. Daphne and Cam stepped around these and made their way to the desk overflowing with files, a small bronze bust, a golden medallion, two hand-painted plates, and the old-fashioned record player. The record player was propped open and was playing opera music at a low volume.

"Follow me," the doctor said, removing the needle from the album. Then she led them through another door into a much larger, more orderly, room. Dr. Lee Reynolds sat behind a desk along one wall, and he nodded at them as they entered.

It was dark and cold, and the lights flickering from the enormous grid of monitors along the back wall gave the impression of walking into a lightning storm without sound or rain. As Daphne looked more carefully at the twenty-inch surveillance monitors lined up like a chess board, she began to recognize the places—the pool, the ballroom, the beach, the ancient oak tree, the pier at Willows Anchorage, Bowen Point, Laguna Beach, Christy Ranch, and—Daphne swallowed hard—the stream in Central Valley. With a sinking feeling, she realized the cameras had been trained on her the whole time she'd tried to drown herself.

"This is how Prospero knows everything that happens on this island," Dr. Gray said with an air of grandeur. "There's always someone here, watching. We want our patients to be safe, and we want the exercises to run smoothly."

Daphne's attention was caught by the sight of her parents entering their unit. She couldn't hear what they were saying but could see the concern on their faces as they sat in the two striped chairs and put their feet up. Her father was complaining, probably about having to go to the ball, and her mother was rolling her eyes and barely tolerating it.

"What about privacy?" Daphne asked as her father unbuttoned the top of his pants to make himself more comfortable.

"Your modesty is sweet," Dr. Gray replied. "But this is science. This is important work. There is no such thing as privacy when it comes to saving lives. This is surgery for the soul."

Heat rushed with full force across Daphne's cheeks as she thought of someone watching her and Brock. "Are these cameras in every unit?"

At that moment a door opened on the opposite wall of Dr. Reynolds, and Mary Ellen entered. "Excuse me. Am I interrupting?"

"I'll call you back in a minute," Hortense Gray said.

"Shall I step out, too, then?" Lee asked.

"If you don't mind," Hortense replied. "This won't take long."

Lee stepped out of a door behind his desk, which Daphne saw led to his office. So he, Mary Ellen, and Hortense all had offices leading to the surveillance room. Daphne wondered if Mary Ellen was also a psychologist of some kind.

When Daphne and Cam were left alone in the room with Hortense, the doctor said, "I sent for you because there is something I want you to see."

"Oh?" Daphne noticed Brock diving into the pool.

"We have a new arrival. His name is Giovanni."

"Cam mentioned him."

Hortense Gray arched a brow and then glared at Cam. "Is that so?"

Daphne wished she hadn't said anything. Now Cam was in trouble.

"I just told her that he arrived. I didn't share any sensitive information."

"I see." Hortense pointed to one of the screens. "No matter. Look here. Put on these headphones and have a listen."

A dozen headphones covered the desk in front of the computer monitors. Hortense put on a pair, and Daphne and Cam followed suit. The doctor pulled a switch, and sound came over the phones.

Giovanni sat on the chalky bluff, on the ground, across from Bridget, who bathed in the sun on her belly in her pink bikini. She tugged at a few weeds and twisted them in her fingers. The sun blazed down on them, and the wind whipped her blonde hair to one side of her face. Giovanni's dark eyes were trained on her through the dark wavy hair that fell across his brow.

"So why did you do it?" Bridget asked.

"Do what?"

"*It?*"

Giovanni licked his lips and threw his head back. "Man, let me guess. You don't mean the drugs."

She shook her head.

"You don't want to know."

"Of course, I do. Please?"

He looked over her beautiful body and then closed his eyes and sighed. "I was fourteen. There was this girl."

"I thought so."

"My foster parents, they were really religious, you know?"

She nodded.

"They didn't understand that I couldn't share their beliefs. They put me in a Christian school and took me to church, but, man, if there's a God, I don't really want to have anything to do with him, you know?"

Bridget didn't reply. She watched him and waited.

"And I know he doesn't want to have anything to do with me."

"Why would you say such a thing?" Bridget asked.

"'Cause I'm no good." He smiled, as though he were proud of that fact.

"Of course, you're good. We all have some good in us, somewhere. *I* think so, anyway."

"Nah. God has favorites, and I'm not one of them."

Bridget sat up and moved closer to Giovanni. "I don't believe that."

"Well, anyway…" He kind of laughed.

"Go on. Tell me."

"So, I liked this girl from my school," he continued. "And one day, right before spring break, I got her number from a friend of mine, and I texted her."

"What did you say?"

His face turned red. "I was trying to be cool, I guess."

Bridget waited.

"I had never said a word to her. Not one. I was so stupid back then."

"Everybody does stupid things."

"I said something dirty to her. Real bad."

She laughed. "So? Do you think you're the only boy to ever do that?"

Daphne was shocked to see how red his face was, even beneath his dark complexion.

"She showed it to her mom."

"Oh, no."

"Then her mom called my foster mom."

"Not cool at all."

"Before that, no one trusted me enough to give me my own cell phone. I blew it, man."

"We all make mistakes."

"I was mortified. Up to that point, my religious foster mom thought I was a good kid. She was always saying how good I was. No one ever thought that of me before."

"I doubt that's true."

"It is. Really. My real parents didn't want me." He crossed his arms and said, "Ah, forget it. I don't want a pity party."

"I just wanted to know why you did it." Bridget stretched out on her back and put her hands behind her head. Daphne felt a little jealous of her beauty. "Everybody who comes to this place has a story to tell. So you did it because you were embarrassed?"

"I don't want to talk about this anymore."

"That's kind of a silly reason to want to end everything."

Daphne jerked her head back with surprise. Why would Bridget say such a thing?

"You don't get it," Giovanni said.

"Then tell me," Bridget said, not looking at him. Her eyes were closed against the bright sun.

Giovanni shook his head and punched a hand with a fist. "I let down the only person that ever believed in me. Now, can we change the subject?"

"But you and your foster mom got past that eventually. Didn't you?"

Tears formed in Giovanni's eyes. "She had cancer. It wasn't long after that…"

"Oh, no. I'm so sorry." Bridget sat up. "But you made your peace?"

Giovanni nodded. "I guess. Though I sometimes think that…" he stopped.

"What?"

"Never mind."

"Tell me."

He looked up into the bright sky and sighed. Then he shook his head and murmured, "Maybe she wouldn't have gotten so sick if…"

"How could it have been your fault?"

"I exasperated her. I wore her out."

"No, Giovanni," Bridget said sternly. "Look at me."

Daphne's mouth dropped open when Bridget leaned in and kissed Giovanni on the lips—not on the cheek, and not a quick peck, but a full mouth-on-mouth kiss. Daphne glanced at Cam, whose eyes fell to the floor.

Before Daphne could react, she was drawn back to the screen and to Giovanni's tears. Then Bridget jumped up from the ground and grabbed Giovanni's hand, leading him to the edge of the bluff.

"Let's jump," she dared.

He looked out at the raging sea below. "You're crazy."

"So? It'll be fun. Come on. I've done it before. The secret is to jump way out. You can't go straight down, or you'll be bashed into the rocks. But if you leap way out, it's amazing."

"No thanks." He turned away from the edge, wiping his eyes.

She twirled around to face him. "Oh, come on! It's such a thrill!"

Then, while he faced away from her, Bridget climbed down the edge of the cliff so that only the upper half of her face and hands were visible. She clung to the ledge and screamed.

Daphne was startled and shrieked, then blushed with embarrassment when the doctor and Cam glanced her way.

Giovanni rushed to the edge and grabbed Bridget's hand.

"I slipped! Don't let me fall!" Bridget shouted. "Oh, God! Oh, God!"

Giovanni pulled Bridget to safety. They were both breathing rapidly, as though they'd run a mile. Tears poured down Bridget's cheeks. She wrapped her arms around him and wept against his chest, thanking him again and again for saving her life.

She was a really talented actress, Daphne thought.

The doctor removed her headphones and smiled at Daphne. "The boy feels better about himself already."

"But is it wise to lead him on like that?" Daphne asked. "A broken heart might make him worse."

"Cameron, would you leave us, please?"

Cam nodded and left the room. Daphne felt less comfortable now that she was alone with the doctor.

"I want you to see something," Dr. Gray said. She went to the desk and pressed the lighted button on her dashboard. After a few moments, she pressed another. Then she pointed to the same screen they had just been watching, only, this time, it was Cam with Bridget. "This was filmed last summer, Cam's first day here with us."

Bridget lay on her towel on the bluff in the same pink bikini twirling a strand of grass between her fingers. Cam stretched out on another towel. Unlike Giovanni, Cam was sunbathing, too. He looked thinner back then and was as white as a sheet.

"This feels nice," Cam said. "Thanks for bringing me to this spot."

"Isn't this the best?" Bridget asked in a dreamy voice.

"If you mean being here with you, then yes," he said, making Daphne want to gag.

How corny, she thought.

"What's your story, anyway?" Bridget asked. "I was just told that you're going through rehab."

"That's all there is to it," Cam replied.

"But why drugs? What draws you to them?" Bridget pressed. She rolled onto her side and propped up her head with one hand, looking down at Cam. "You're so beautiful, you know that? How could someone so beautiful contaminate himself?"

Daphne could see Cam's jaw muscles flexing as he gritted his teeth.

"Just wanted to have fun," Cam said. "I was dumb, that's all."

"I don't believe you. There's more to you than that. I can tell."

Cam sat up and looked up and down her beautiful body.

"Has anyone ever told you how much you resemble the young Carrie Fisher?" he asked.

"Who?" Bridget asked.

So she wasn't a *Star Wars* fan, Daphne thought.

"You know. Princess Lea?" Cam explained.

Bridget held up one hand and gave the Vulcan greeting from *Star Trek*. "Live long and prosper."

Cam slapped his forehead. "Now I know we could never be together."

Bridget laughed and playfully shoved him. "So you use humor to mask your true feelings," she said, a little too casually, Daphne thought.

"What do you want from me?" Cam asked with a half-laugh. "Blood?"

"I'll leave that to the ghosts that wander the island," Bridget teased. Then she added, "Most people who get addicted to drugs don't have much self-worth. Do you think that's true of you?"

He shrugged. "Never gave it much thought."

"Do you have any passions, any major interests?"

"Comic books, movies, novels—mostly sci-fi and fantasy."

"You like to escape."

"Exactly."

"Because?"

"Some worlds are better than this one, I guess."

Bridget jumped to her feet. The sun was beginning to set, and the sky was full of glorious pinks and purples. "What about all this beauty?" She swept her arms open to the sky.

Cam kept his eyes focused on Bridget, and a shiver of jealousy ran down Daphne's back. He didn't reply.

"Don't your parents love you?" Bridget asked. "That's why most kids turn to drugs. They feel unloved."

"I think I'm getting burned," Cam said evasively as he climbed to his feet. "I need to get out of this sun."

"But it's going down," she protested.

"Not soon enough."

Bridget took his hand and led him to the edge. "Let's jump in!"

Cam looked out over the raging sea below. He shrugged and said, "Okay."

"Be sure to leap out as far as you can," she said. "You don't want to get bashed into those rocks below."

"You sound like you've done this before."

"Yep! And it's amazing. Ready?"

She held his hand and counted to three, and then the two of them leapt out into the sea.

Daphne held her breath.

Another camera provided a new angle of them flying over the edge and down toward the water. When they popped back up, Bridget screamed.

"Help me, Cam! Oh my God! Help me!"

The camera followed Cam as he swam to Bridget's side.

"What happened? Are you okay?"

Blood spilled from Bridget's arm as she held it up and floundered in the water. "I think I broke my wrist. Oh my god, it hurts! And I can't keep myself up!"

Daphne couldn't tell this time if Bridget was acting or truly injured as the flailing girl sunk beneath the surface. Cam wrapped an arm across her as she collapsed and fell limp. Daphne watched on as Cam towed Bridget to the beach and carried her up the steps of the boardwalk as fast as he could, with the same look of intensity on his face and the same heavy breathing as Daphne had just witnessed in Giovanni.

Hortense Gray flipped a switch and removed her headphones. Daphne took hers off, too, wondering why the doctor had decided to show this to her.

"Everything I do serves an important purpose," Dr. Gray explained. "I want you to remember that."

Daphne didn't know what to say.

"The patients in my charge are suffering, and I help them learn to love themselves, which in turn allows them to love life."

"But…" Daphne started to ask again about Bridget's role and the possibility of broken hearts, but the doctor continued.

"Cam's father abandoned him when he was a young boy, and although he adjusted adequately throughout grade school, his lack of self-worth raised its ugly head when he became a man and left for the university." She returned her headphones to her ears and said, "There's one more thing I want you to see."

Daphne put the headphones on and stared at the screen, feeling a bit like Ebenezer Scrooge with the Ghost of Christmas Past.

CHAPTER SEVEN

Giovanni at Christy Ranch

Daphne descended the stairs from the second floor of the main building to the lobby, thinking about the videos the doctor had shown her. The last one had been Cam's Limuw ceremony. His biological father had come along with his mother and stepfather. It had been heart-wrenching to watch Cam face off with the father who had abandoned him.

In the weeks after his ceremony, Cam had recovered by having revenge on his father. Daphne didn't see any of that footage. According to Hortense, he eventually reconciled with all three parents and devoted himself to helping the doctor on the island.

As Daphne thought more about what the doctor had said, and as she reflected on her own progress with her parents and Brock, she thought she might like to volunteer, too, after her parents and Brock's therapy was finished. It must be a good feeling to know you helped other people.

When she stepped from the foyer out into the bright sunshine, Cam was waiting for her. Now why wasn't she surprised?

He thrust his palms up to her and said, "You don't have to tell me. That's not why I waited."

"Okay."

They started walking toward the pool.

"I don't even want to know," he added.

"Fine."

"She showed you my scene with Bridget, didn't she," he said without inflection.

"I thought you didn't want to know."

"I don't."

She jerked her thumb toward the pool, where Brock was swimming laps. "He'll be doing that for a while."

"Good." Cam took both her hands. "Because there's something you might want to see."

He had a strange smile on his face, like a kid about to play a joke.

"Okay." She shrugged. "What?"

"Giovanni's about to take the horse-riding excursion. Come with?"

Daphne frowned. "I don't know."

Cam put his hands on his hips with a look of exasperation. "Oh, come on! You'd get to be a watcher."

Daphne lifted her chin, her curiosity piqued. As much as she hated getting thrown off of Pearl, she was rather eager to see what it was like to be a watcher. Hortense had assured her getting bucked off had been a fluke. And it would be thrilling to see Giovanni's reaction to the exercise. Even more exciting would be the opportunity to see more of how everything worked on this island.

A smile crossed her lips. "Well, alright."

"Great!" He fist-bumped her. "Get changed into better shoes—good for running—and meet up at the jeeps in half an hour."

Her heart thumped with anticipation as the group of trail riders journeyed in the jeeps to the stables. As she pulled her new scarf lower on her forehead, her fingers were literally shaking with excitement. Vince and Dave rode with her and Cam, while Bridget, Giovanni, and Philip rode with Roger. Kelly met them at the gate as Roger drove off.

Daphne wondered why Roger always drove to each excursion. Surely someone else participating in the trail ride could drive and save him the time. Daphne's thoughts were soon interrupted, however, when Kelly asked her to mount a red mare named Scout. A little wave of excitement shot through her veins. Giovanni was riding *Pearl*.

Scout was drastically different from Pearl. Where Pearl bit and fidgeted and constantly vied for the position near the front, Scout seemed to know her place, and that was near the end of the line. Daphne said as much to Cam, who replied in a whisper that Pearl was trained to be aggressive, in order to make her rider nervous. Daphne's mouth dropped open. Cam winked.

At the top of Mount Diablo, the group gazed out at the beautiful sea, searching for humpbacks. Daphne sipped on her water bottle, enjoying herself so much more this time around. She took in the fresh sea air, listened to the song of the gulls flying overhead, and clapped her hands when two humpbacks finally showed themselves. Yet, despite her enjoyment, she felt uneasy for Giovanni. She hoped he wouldn't get bucked off as she had.

Bridget seemed to have no trouble giving Giovanni her attention and charm, and Daphne was surprised by Cam's indifference. She supposed he knew it was just an act and wasn't threatened by it.

Dave, as always, entertained them with an ongoing monologue that was hit or miss in the humor department. Daphne did have to laugh when he told Vince he looked like a skinny Shrek on a fat Donkey.

Her heart picked up speed as they began their descent down the mountain, and Pearl, as if on cue, refused to cooperate for Giovanni. Daphne glanced back at the poor guy, who repeatedly shouted, "Giddyup, girl!"

Cam nudged her with his boot and said softly, "Follow me."

Kelly led them at a trot down the mountain. Though the fast pace was exuberating, Daphne clung to the saddle horn. They topped the canyon ridge over Central Valley where Roger was waiting in his jeep. Cam, Vince, and Dave dismounted, waving to her to do the same, and handed their reins over to Kelly, Philip, and Bridget. Daphne and the three boys then squeezed into the jeep with Roger.

So Roger drove so he could be on standby for the watchers?

"Where are we going?" she asked, hemmed in between Cam and Vince in the backseat.

"The west side of the island," Cam said.

"The haunted side," Roger added with a wink.

Roger drove them along the canyon ridge past the resort, around Central Valley toward the base of Sierra Blanca where they came upon a sign on a wooden post that read, "Chumash Ruins/Christy Ranch" with an arrow pointing right and "Sierra Blanca" with an arrow pointing left. Roger passed the sign and parked the jeep behind a massive grotto.

"Now, you've got to be stone quiet," Cam warned. "Just stay behind me and do what I do."

Daphne nodded, her heart beating fast. She couldn't wait to discover what would happen next.

They hiked down the bluff, where the grass was as high as Daphne's hips. Like leopards in the Serengeti, they crouched and crept stealthily toward what Daphne now realized was Stan's orange and gray dome tent. They stopped about thirty feet away from it.

Cam whispered, "This is where we were when you finally decided to go to the tent."

Dave chuckled. "You had us nervous."

"Why?" she asked.

"Looked like you weren't going for it," Dave explained. "One of us almost had to enter the game."

"There he is," Roger said, pointing. "Hold still."

Pearl galloped like a horse from the gate in a race for the win as Giovanni hung on for dear life. When the horse reached the tent, it came to a halt and snorted.

Stan emerged and grabbed Pearl's reins. "Whoa, girl."

"Thank God," the boy said breathlessly.

"That's a good girl." Stan slipped a treat into her mouth. "What happened, man?" he asked Giovanni.

He fought for his breath. "I got left behind by the group. And then this horse went crazy on me." Giovanni dismounted and took several steps away from Pearl.

"Sorry to hear that, kiddo."

"Can you help me find my way back?" Giovanni sounded urgent.

"Sure, sure. No problem." Stan tied Pearl to the nearest tree. "They're probably looking for you. Why don't we give them time to find you, and if they don't in the next hour, I'll pack up my camp and guide you back?"

"Thanks, man." Giovanni followed Stan into the tent.

Cam turned to Daphne. "Now we get to have some fun. Come on."

They crept to the tree and untied Pearl.

At that moment, an island fox scurried down the rocks across the valley toward the tent.

"Hold on," Daphne whispered. "Is that Mini-me?"

"Yep," Roger answered. "Wave as you pass by the little fella. The doc will get a kick out of it."

With Pearl in tow, the group ran past the tent, down the grassy hill, each giving the fox a friendly wave. It was fun to be part of this elaborate plan—whatever it was. They heard Giovanni's shouts about the horse getting away as they rounded a boulder. Adrenaline surged through her when Christy Ranch came into view. The bunkhouse, bridge, and ranch house looked exactly as they had a few days ago. Although she was excited and having fun, seeing the place again gave Daphne the willies.

They crossed Haunted Bridge, the ravine below deeper than Daphne had imagined. Vince took Pearl around the back as the others entered the farmhouse. Daphne was amazed by what she found inside. People, props, a wardrobe, chairs and mirrors—all resembling the bustling backstage of a Broadway theater. Bridget, Gregory, and Emma were there as well as Pete and another man in his thirties whom Daphne had not yet met. Cam introduced him as Marty and explained he was the make-up artist and acting coach.

"How would you like to enter the game, young lady?" Marty asked, motioning for her to sit in the dressing-room style chair he was standing beside.

"I thought *I* was going in this time," Dave complained.

"Dr. Gray just called and said to let Daphne have a turn, if she wants," Pete said. He turned to Daphne. "You'd basically go in doing what I did during your therapy—scary face in the window tonight, and then scared-out-of-your-mind runaway in the morning."

"Think you can handle that?" Marty asked with a smile.

Daphne glanced at Cam.

"You'd have a blast," he said with an encouraging nod. "It's up to you, though."

"What if I mess up?" she asked.

"Heavens no," Marty said. "That won't happen."

"Marty will give you some tips," Emma chimed in. "He's a great coach."

"We've all learned from him," Cam said.

The somewhat effeminate make-up artist took a slight bow. "At your service, dearie."

Roger stepped toward her. "You can't really mess up in this here game, Daphne, unless you break the illusion. There's no right or wrong other than that one rule. Alright?"

"Alright," she said.

"Think you're ready?" Greg asked.

How could she not give it a try? It was like entering the most amazing amusement park on the face of the earth. "I think so."

"If you lose your confidence, you can always run away and come back here," Marty assured her. "We can send someone else in, then."

"Like me," said Dave, who was obviously eager to go into the game himself.

"Well?" Bridget asked her.

Everyone looked at Daphne expectantly.

"I'll do it," she said.

While Emma and Bridget combed through the wardrobe for the right dingy clothes for her to wear, Marty created the illusion of dark circles beneath Daphne's eyes. He also added white powder to make her look dusty and dirty.

"Put your bracelet in your pocket for now," he told her. "It will give you away."

Bridget underwent a similar transformation, as Emma and Cam helped her into a white Victorian-style dress.

"You were the ghost!" Daphne said as Marty put the finishing touches on her face.

"That's me," Bridget said, smiling. "Though we take turns—Emma and I."

After Daphne's costume was complete—raggedy jeans that were a bit too big and a grimy t-shirt (plus her new scarf, which she refused to remove)—Marty and the others gave her acting tips.

"You haven't eaten for two full days, and you're famished," Marty said. "You're also scared out of your mind because you fear for your life."

"Show her how to do the shakes," Roger instructed Pete.

Pete transformed into the terrified man she had met the morning after she had stayed in the bunkhouse. "You don't want to go overboard. Just a little shaky, like you're too weak to keep yourself stable."

Everyone there showed her how they had played the same part she was about to take on, and they laughed at one another, going in and out of character. Daphne had never been around a more fun and exhilarating group of people.

"Stan just twisted his ankle," Vince said from the window, where he stood with binoculars. "Giovanni is taking the backpack to the bunkhouse."

The energy in the room was incredible.

"You'll enter the game at dusk," Roger said. "Why don't we eat while we wait?"

The group then set about pulling food from the fridge in the kitchen, just off the main room: lunchmeat, cheeses, condiments, sliced tomatoes and cucumbers, and big hoagie buns. They had sandwiches with chips and dips and cut up fruit and veggies. Pete brewed a pot of tea and a pot of coffee. Someone—maybe Vince—turned on a television monitor in the living room where they could all see what was going on in the bunkhouse. Stan was manipulating Giovanni into opening up by first talking about his own problems.

When dusk finally came, Daphne was eager to get started.

Roger put a fatherly hand on her shoulder. "If you get caught tonight, just improvise."

"Get caught?" she asked.

"Sometimes they stay inside and cower in fear, and sometimes they come after you," he explained, dropping his hand. "Everyone's different."

"Just don't break character," Marty said.

"And no matter what happens," Pete said, "do not admit it's a game. You never want to break the illusion."

Everyone in the room exchanged uneasy glances at Pete's warning.

"What would happen if I did?" Daphne asked, uneasy now herself.

"Never mind that," Roger said. "Just have fun with it, okay?"

Daphne glanced at Cam, who gave her a reassuring smile. "You'll do great."

"Your mission is to be seen in the window," Pete instructed. "Make a little noise so he'll look your way. Then duck and come back here."

"That's when I'll take over," Bridget said.

"There are steps near the bridge," Cam added. "You can hide in the ravine if he comes after you."

"There's a tunnel from there that will bring you back here," Pete said.

"Maybe we should show it to her first," Cam said. "She's never seen it."

"Make it quick," Roger said. "Dusk is falling."

"A tunnel?" Daphne didn't like the sound of that.

"I'll show her," Dave offered.

Daphne followed him to the back of the house. They stepped outside past Pearl to a cellar door, which Dave pulled open before switching on a light.

"You don't have to show me," she said. "I don't need to see it."

"Come on," he insisted.

She followed him down the steps into a cellar and then through another door leading to a dark tunnel.

"This goes all the way to the ravine," Dave said. "It's a straight shot."

She shivered. "It's pitch dark in there."

It also smelled damp and moldy.

"You'll have a flashlight with you," he said. "But if you're too scared, just say the word, and I'll take your place."

"You enjoy this, don't you," she said as he closed the tunnel door and she followed him from the cellar.

"Oh, yeah."

She was glad to be outside in the fresh air and wide, open space again. She took a deep breath.

They returned to the house to find Bridget in full make-up—powdery white from head to toe. "Ready?" she asked Daphne.

"Ready."

Gregory gave her a flashlight, and, as the two girls left the farmhouse, the others called out, "Break a leg!"

Along with dusk, a chill had enveloped the island. Daphne and Bridget ran across the grass to Haunted Bridge and giggled together as they crossed the deep ravine.

"I'll wait for you here," Bridget said.

Daphne gave her a nervous glance.

"Don't be scared," she added. "Just have fun. Oh, and one more thing. The bullets in Stan's gun are real, so don't let yourself get shot."

"Yeah, right," Daphne said, laughing.

"Seriously."

Daphne's mouth dropped open. "Why on earth are there real bullets in his gun?"

"Dr. Gray said blanks would break the illusion. But don't worry. Stan knows what he's doing. It's just occasionally a patient grabs the gun and goes postal on us."

Daphne's mouth went dry. "Isn't that a bit risky?"

"There are only two bullets loaded," she said. "Your chances of getting a lethal hit from one of them are next to nothing. Plus, it adds to the thrill. Now go on."

The excitement that had been coursing through her veins was now replaced by legitimate fear as she jogged down the hill toward the bunkhouse. She could have refused to continue, but she wanted to do it. It was crazy, mad, insane, but she was having the time of her life. As she neared the dusty window, alight from the glow of Stan's lantern inside, Daphne was terrified but grateful to be alive.

A noise behind her made her turn. The little island fox stood five yards away beneath a scrawny tree. Daphne winked at the camera on the end of the fox's tail and then turned back to the window. She could hear Giovanni talking.

How could she get him to the window? She scoured around the ground until her eyes fell on an overturned metal bucket. She scooped up a handful of pea gravel, and threw the pebbles, one at a time, at the bucket.

It became quiet inside. They were listening. She threw a few more pebbles, her face close to the window. Someone moved toward her. As soon as she saw Giovanni, Daphne ducked around the side of the house. The door opened, and she heard him run out, looking in all directions.

"Who's there!" he shouted. "Show yourself!"

Daphne pressed her back against the side of the house, breathing rapidly. Giovanni was now between her and the bridge, so she needed to wait for him to return to the house before she could take off for the farmhouse. She held her breath and froze, listening. She nearly wet her pants when Giovanni came around the corner and grabbed her.

"Who are you? And what are you up to?" he demanded.

On the end of his shaky hand, the gun pointed directly at her.

CHAPTER EIGHT

Gunshots

"You have to help me," she said, recalling what Roger and the others had said about improvising. She shook without acting, terrified and excited at the same time.

"Who are you?" he said, unconvinced.

"Daphne. I came here for therapy. But things…they got out of hand…it became too weird…so I ran away." She looked to her left and then to her right. "Are you here alone?"

"No. Another guy's with me."

"Do you trust him?"

"Don't know yet. Are you saying I should trust you?" He squeezed her upper arm so hard that she winced.

"I'm starving. I don't care if you trust me or not, but I'll do anything you say for just a bite of food."

He looked her up and down. "Were you the one screaming on the bridge?"

She wasn't sure what to say, but she knew if she hesitated too long, he'd lose any trust in her she might have gained. "No. I don't know what that was, but I don't believe in ghosts."

The front door creaked open, and Stan limped around the corner. "What's going on out here?"

Before either Giovanni or Daphne could reply, the shrill scream blasted through the darkening sky once again from Haunted Bridge. Giovanni took off running for it.

"Stop him," Stan muttered.

"Why can't you?"

He pointed to his ankle. "I can't."

"Wait!" Daphne called out, running after Giovanni.

She could barely see in the blanket of darkness that had descended on the island, but the moon was bright enough for her to make out Giovanni's figure stopped about fifty yards from the ravine, the gun pointed at the ghostly figure of Bridget. Before Daphne could reach him, he fired twice.

"No!" she screamed.

When she caught up to him, he was searching the bottom of the ravine from the bridge. Daphne looked down, unable to see clearly because of the shadows. Her stomach was in knots, her throat pinched closed. She could barely breathe. Where had Bridget gone?

"Why would you fire at something when you didn't know what it was?" Daphne screamed.

"It was a ghost," Giovanni said. "I saw her. The wife of that slave trader. Haven't you heard the legend?"

"If she's a ghost, then why shoot her?" Daphne asked. "She's already dead."

"It got her to leave, didn't it?" he said angrily. "What else was I supposed to do?"

Daphne looked all around but saw no trace of Bridget. She only hoped she had made it out safely. Maybe she was in the tunnel on her way to the farmhouse and not at the bottom of the ravine.

As tempted as she was to end the game to discover what had happened to her friend, she remembered the warning the others had given. They had said, no matter what, she wasn't to break the illusion. Plus, the sooner she lured Giovanni away from here, the sooner a rescue mission, if needed, could commence.

"Let's get out of here before she comes back," Daphne said.

She ran toward the bunkhouse and was relieved when Giovanni followed.

As she and Giovanni collapsed on the two wooden chairs, Giovanni said, "What if that was another one of their weird games? What if I shot a real person?"

Daphne glanced across the room at Stan, who turned and limped out to the screened porch to sit in the wooden rocker. He looked too upset to speak.

"It doesn't matter," Daphne said, since Stan had said nothing. "Whether it was a real ghost or one of *them*, we have to get off this island. Those people are dangerous."

"You really think so?" Giovanni asked.

"I was almost killed when a horse bucked me off," she said, looking him straight in the eye. "What kind of therapy risks people's lives?"

Giovanni nodded. "This girl named Bridget nearly fell off a cliff, then my elevator dropped three floors, and now this? I don't know what to think."

"I say we head to Scorpion Anchorage first thing in the morning," Daphne said. "That's the best way off this island. There are other people over there. Regular, normal people. Don't you agree, Stan?"

"You will have to go without me. My ankle's busted."

"We can't leave you behind, man," Giovanni said.

"I've got a horse," Daphne said. "I found her wandering around."

"Is she white?" Giovanni asked.

Daphne nodded. "Why?"

"She's crazy. You can't trust her."

"You two go for help," Stan said. "I'll hide out here and wait. I've got plenty of food and water. I'm too sore to travel."

"Wait a minute!" Giovanni scrutinized Daphne's face. "How did you know his name was Stan?"

"You told me."

"No, I didn't."

Daphne's face turned red. "I don't know. I guess I met him before or something." She gave Stan an anxious look that said *help me.*

"I thought you looked familiar," Stan said. "We met on the beach about a week ago. You were with that guy named Cam."

"Oh, that's right."

Giovanni studied her. "Should we get started now, for the east end?"

She lifted her brows in surprise. "Now? Why not wait until morning?"

"They'll be out looking for me in the morning," Giovanni said.

Daphne glanced at Stan, who said, "Sounds like a good idea to me."

She wasn't ready to run the game alone. She'd already messed up twice—once by getting caught and again by saying Stan's name. Ugh. Why was Stan encouraging her to go? The only reasonable explanation was that someone else would enter the game and take it over. Maybe it was Daphne's job to lead Giovanni to him or her.

"Is there a certain path I should take?" Daphne asked Stan.

"Follow the stream in Central Valley," he said. "It will take you all the way to the naval road. From there, follow the road to Scorpion Anchorage."

After eating a can of nuts and taking two of Stan's canteens of water, Daphne and Giovanni crept from the bunkhouse in the dead of night and headed for the east side of the island. Adrenaline ran through Daphne's veins. As excited as she felt, she had no idea what to expect.

They followed the small circle of her flashlight up the grassy slope from Christy Ranch. The wind chilled Daphne, and she had to admit she was feeling sleepy, not having expected to be traipsing across the island during the night. She was surprised by how loud the crickets and other insects sounded. The island was teeming with bugs, and they were part of a far-reaching orchestra.

"Central Valley should be on the other side of these hills," she told Giovanni.

"You sound like you know a lot about this island," he said with what sounded like suspicion.

"I should," she said. "I've been wandering it alone for two days."

"Then why were you on the west end if you think the east is the way off?"

"I thought I could flag down a boat over at Kinton Point, but I waited several hours yesterday and had no luck."

Then she added, "Plus I was hungry, so when I saw you and that other guy running to the bunkhouse, I was hoping I could get a bit of food."

Giovanni didn't say more as they made their way over the hills and into Central Valley. It was slow moving in the dark, with only the small circle of light to guide them. The stars were brilliant overhead, and the moon helped them to see the outlines of the distant hills and shrubs, and Sierra Blanca to their right and Mount Diablo to their left, but the ground outside of their little light was in shadows. After some time, she heard the soft rush of the stream running over rocks. The smell, too, was unmistakably fresh. She half-skipped and half danced with her arm through Giovanni's.

"Here it is!" she said. "I was afraid I'd get us lost. Thank God!"

"So now we just follow it to the road?" he asked.

"I guess so."

They continued walking.

"About how long do you think it will take?" he asked.

"Not sure. Three or four hours, maybe?"

She doubted they would get very far before something new would happen, and because of this, she was jumpy.

"So why are you here?" Giovanni asked, after they'd walked in silence for several minutes.

"Oh, I guess for the same reason most people come here." She really didn't want to talk about it. Her therapy was over. He was the one that needed to talk. But he kept after her until, before she knew it, she was relaying the story about Kara and Joey, and how she had heard and done nothing to save her sister's life, but how she might not have been able to do anything to stop it anyway. She even told him about the Prozac and the Tylenol, and a bit about Brock.

He asked if she had cancer. This took her by surprise until she realized the scarf probably made him think she had lost her hair to chemotherapy.

"Yes," she lied.

"Sorry."

She was surprised by how much he told her when she had finished. As they trudged across rocks, over grass, through shrubbery, and all manner of landscape, he told her about how alone he felt in the universe, where not a single person was truly devoted to him and his well-being.

"Someone must have paid for you to come here," she said. "Who were you living with before you came to the island?"

"This older, wealthy couple," he said. "I think they're helping me because they're goody two-shoes, not because they really care about *me*. They don't even know *me*."

"Maybe *you* have to be the one person in the universe devoted to you and to your well-being," she said. "Maybe you have to be the first one, anyway. After that, then others will follow."

He stopped in his tracks. She thought of snakes, lizards, mice, and all kinds of possible reasons.

"What is it?" she asked, heart thumping.

"Nothing," he said. "Come on, let's keep moving."

They hadn't gone on much farther when, just as the anticipation of something happening had begun to wane and leave Daphne feeling disappointed, something happened. A loud snarl echoed across the hills—from what direction, Daphne couldn't tell.

"What was that?" she whispered.

"Dunno. Don't move. Switch off the light."

Daphne did as he said. If she could know for certain that the snarl was made by a person and not an animal, she might be able to control her trembling. She took Giovanni's hand.

A few seconds later, the snarl came again—this time louder and closer. She held her breath as twigs snapped and pebbles crushed together, indications that something was moving toward them. Then Giovanni slipped the flashlight from her shaking hand and switched it on, pointing it directly at…what?

The flashlight dropped at her feet and Giovanni took off running, leaving her alone with the thing. She followed Giovanni, screaming at the top of her lungs. The only thing she could think of to describe what she saw was, "Big Foot."

As she stumbled along the stream after Giovanni, she assured herself that it was a person in a costume. A real creature of that magnitude couldn't exist on this small of an island. Nevertheless, she ran, just in case.

Then the thing grabbed her arm, and she let out a rueful cry. "God! God!"

"Daphne, it's me," came a familiar voice.

She stopped, breathless, and turned toward the creature.

"Philip," he said. "Come with me."

"Oh, thank goodness," Daphne struggled to catch her breath. "Do you know if Bridget's alright?"

"She's fine. Not a scratch." He walked her to a jeep parked behind some shrubs.

"What now?" she asked him, full of relief.

He climbed behind the wheel. "Did you have fun?"

"Oh, yeah! It was a blast!" And that was no lie.

"Hortense wants him to wander around alone for a while, so he can find himself."

She wondered how that would pan out for Giovanni. "So where are we headed?"

"Back to the resort. You need your sleep. We have another big day ahead of us tomorrow. You, especially."

She jerked back her head. "Why me especially?"

"It's a surprise."

The lights of the resort came into view. Philip dropped her off at her cabana. Inside, she found Brock waiting for her.

"What in the world happened to you?" he asked.

She smiled, wishing she could tell him all about it. "I, um, was just trying out different costumes for tomorrow's ball. Do you likey?"

"Not at all."

She wasn't a very good actress. She was going to have to step up her game if she was really going to have her revenge.

CHAPTER NINE

Costume Ball Disaster

The next evening, after a relatively uneventful day, Daphne dressed alone in her room for the masquerade ball. She studied her reflection in the bathroom mirror and checked out the beautiful costume—a long white Victorian style dress, a white-blonde wig that fell in ringlets on her shoulders, and a wreath of pearls around her head. Pinned to the front of the bodice was a cream-colored piece of fabric in the shape of a scroll, and embroidered in swirly letters, was the last line from Lord Tennyson's poem:

The web was woven curiously,
The charm is broken utterly,
Draw near and fear not,—this is I,
The Lady of Shalott.

It had been Cam's idea. Daphne had never even heard of The Lady of Shalott until, after lunch, when they went to see the doctor's collection, Cam had pulled the gown and accessories from the closet, reciting the entire ballad by memory. Her parents had been off in another dressing room, but Brock had been there with her to hear it. At the end of it, Brock, who had been tinkering with a Batman costume, clapped. Daphne remembered why she used to call her friend "Cam the Ham."

Cam took a bow and then noticed the costume Brock had in his hands. "Please don't tell me you're wearing that Batsuit."

Brock held it up and studied it. "Why not?"

"Everybody knows that the real DC Batsuit utility belt had pockets," Cam said.

Daphne giggled. That was her Cam: the nerd who knew everything about every fantasy universe ever created. She turned to Brock. "Shouldn't you go as my Sir Lancelot, anyway?"

"The poem didn't sound like much of a romance," Brock scoffed. "The knight barely notices the lady, and she languishes in the bottom of a boat."

"But you gotta admit it's a cool costume," Cam said with his charming smile.

In the end, Daphne convinced Brock to go as Lancelot, even though he complained that the knight was just another tragic character who dies.

"Isn't our reason for being here to learn to accept death and to appreciate life?" she had challenged, and that had been the end of it. She hadn't admitted that her main reason for wanting to go as the Lady of Shalott was the beautiful wig.

Now she slipped on a pair of boots—the floor-length full skirt covered them anyway—and headed for Brock's room.

On the way, she ran into Stan, whom she had to admit made a mighty fine Zorro, but she was still a little irked for his part in the cutting of her calf during the staged shark attack. He might be willing to cut himself for the sake of the therapy, but that didn't mean he could do it to her, too. She hadn't been able to ask him anything about it at Christy Ranch, but now she wanted him to know she hadn't appreciated it.

"Any word on Giovanni?" she whispered.

"Not now." He took her hand, and, in character, kissed it, before continuing in the opposite direction toward the main building, once more giving her no chance to complain about her injury.

Daphne also ran into Cam and Bridget, whom Daphne hugged, saying, "So glad you're okay." They were dressed as Annikin and Padame— not the happiest of endings for those two, either. Behind them were

Tweedle Dee and Tweedle Dum—Vince and Dave. They looked hilarious in their matching striped caps, large white collars, blue bowties, and red pants.

"We'll see you there," Vince said with a wave.

"Contrariwise!" Dave shouted. "She'll see *us* there!"

Daphne shook her head as they moved on. She hadn't even knocked when Brock opened the door.

"Wow," he said, giving her a once over.

"Wow yourself." He looked hotter than hot: her knight in shining armor.

Hand in hand, they made their way to the ballroom.

Daphne couldn't believe the crowd awaiting them at the ball. Where had all these people come from? At least sixty, maybe seventy, most of whom she could not recognize (and it didn't help that the lights were dimmed, and everyone was in costume), walked around the food tables and bar. Two zombies mingled with a human-size apple, Picachu shared drinks with Wonder Woman, an alien made nice with three steampunk characters, and Mario flirted with Katniss Everdeen. None of the members of the younger crowd were there, which was strange, since Daphne had passed them on her way to Brock's. She wondered what they were up to. A few couples—Thing One and Thing Two, Dracula and a vampiress, and a doctor and sexy nurse—danced on a small wooden dance floor near an empty stage where two large speakers sent big band music throughout the ball. On the far end of the room near the back tables, Daphne spotted the mad hatter, A.K.A. Hortense Gray.

"Check out your parents," Brock said of the cowboy and Indian speaking with the doctor.

"Oh my gosh." Her father had merely worn a cowboy hat and boots—not much of a costume. But her mother had on a full Indian headdress, a fringed tan leather jacket, and tall matching boots. She looked young and...happy.

Before Daphne reached her parents, Zorro came up behind her and asked for a dance. She noticed the rest of the regulars were trickling in as well.

"You don't mind, do you?" Stan asked Brock.

"No. Of course not."

Daphne was not much of a dancer. Plus, it was a slow song. How awkward. "I was just on my way to talk to my parents," she said, trying to get out of it.

"One song." Stan widened his eyes in an urgent way that alarmed Daphne.

"Well, alright."

She followed him to the dance floor and stood there awkwardly as he took her in his arms, leaving just a few inches between them.

"Are you doing okay?" he asked.

"My leg hurts." That was a lie. It had already healed, as far as she was concerned.

"Sorry about that, kiddo. Dr. Gray's orders." He twirled her under his arm.

"Do you always do what Dr. Gray says?"

"She has helped a lot of people."

Daphne had nothing to say to that. She had to admit—not aloud but to herself—that she and her parents were a lot closer since the rock lice and the shark attack.

"I want you to know something," Stan said.

Daphne lifted her eyebrows. "What?"

"It's about to get intense."

"Tonight? Here?"

Stan nodded.

"But my dad."

Stan squeezed and relaxed his grip on her hand, making her realize she was clenching his.

"This ball took a lot of planning," Stan said. "Dr. Gray canceled yesterday's exercises for him, but tonight's are still on."

"Great." She hoped her father was up to whatever they had in store for them. "What's the plan?"

Stan grinned. "You'll soon find out."

"Why can't you tell me?"

"I don't even know all the details." He twirled her beneath his arm again. "But listen. No matter what happens. Do not break the illusion. That little cut on your leg in the water the other day was nothing, you understand?"

Daphne's mouth dropped open. "You can't be serious. I didn't sign up for any real pain."

"Not you."

The song ended, but as they walked from the dance floor, she said, "Not my parents. Not even Brock."

"Don't worry, Daph. It's going to be great. You'll see. You'll be so grateful at the end of it. I promise."

They reached Brock and her parents before she could ask more.

The first thing her mother said was a repeat from lunch earlier that day, "Did you take your antibiotic?"

"Yes," she lied. She had totally forgotten but didn't want an earful.

"Nice costume," her father said. "What's the Lady of Shalott?"

Daphne explained the poem to him.

"I remember that one from school, now that you mention it," her mother said.

"And who's this Zorro fellow?" her dad asked.

Daphne re-introduced them. They had already met, but her father hadn't remembered Stan.

"Then maybe you know the answer to my question," her dad said to Stan. "Is that a cash bar?"

"No sir," Stan replied. "You already paid for your drinks with Daphne's tuition."

"Oh, they're included," Joe said with a smile.

"Would you like me to get you something?" Stan offered.

"No, no, that's okay. Thank you. I'll get a drink in a minute."

"Don't wait too long," Stan warned.

"Oh, they go fast, do they?" Joe asked.

"Something like that." Stan winked at Daphne and turned away.

Daphne watched him stroll over to the food table until she could no longer see him among the others. Her heart rate had picked up at his last comment. *Don't wait too long.* Whatever was going to happen was going to happen soon.

"Guess we'll head over for a drink," her father said.

"What was that all about?" Brock asked her once her parents had headed for the bar.

Daphne noticed Emma sitting alone in tears at a nearby table.

"I'll be right back," Daphne said. She left before giving Brock a chance to object.

Emma was dressed as Doctor Who. Her hair was tucked beneath a hat. She wore a brown tweed jacket and dark brown bowtie. She looked adorable, but black mascara streaked down her cheeks, and her brown eyes were red-rimmed.

Daphne sat down beside her and leaned close. "What's wrong?"

"I want off this island, that's what." Emma was trembling.

"Has something happened?"

"Just the same old crap."

"Can you talk about it?"

Emma glanced around the room, then lowered her voice and said, "Dr. Gray has got everyone in this place brainwashed, if you ask me. Even her son."

Daphne bent her brows with concern. She'd already suspected as much, but wasn't it for a good cause? "What makes you say that?"

"She's a controlling witch, that's what. Greg and I just want to be together, but apparently I'm not good enough for him." Emma's voice broke on the last few words as sobs overwhelmed her.

Daphne patted her back. "Who cares what she thinks?"

Emma glared at her through her wet lashes. "Are you serious? Who doesn't?"

"Do *you*?"

"Not anymore." Emma's sobs took over her again. "She's been like a mother to me. I can't believe she's treating me like this." Her lips quivered, teeth chattered.

"If she thinks of you as a daughter, maybe it's weird for her to see you with her son."

Emma shook her head. "I wish that was it. If that *were* it, I could take it. But she's been nothing but cold and rude to me since Greg and I took up with each other last summer. I was serious that day I told you to get off the island while you still can, before she lures you in like the others. I only stayed because of Greg."

"Lures me in?"

"These people *live* here," Emma whispered. "Most of them were patients at one time, but all of them stay for the thrill of the games, and they'll do anything she tells them to do. It's like they worship her." Then she added, "Most of them are wealthy, like you and your family, and they give her all their money. Just wait and see. She'll be hitting up your parents for more."

Daphne glanced up at Brock, who was still standing where she had left him and was joined by Cam and Bridget. Her parents were just now getting their drinks handed to them by the bartender. Over at the entrance, three men dressed as bank robbers came in. They wore cut nylons over their heads, loose clothing, boots, and machine guns strapped across their shoulders.

Their costumes were pretty realistic.

"Who are they?" she asked Emma.

Before Emma could reply, one of the bank robbers pulled the double doors shut as another fired in the air and shouted, "Everyone down!"

Then a ring of *real* bullets shot past Daphne, bursting glass and flower vases. She dropped to the floor between the tables, nearly losing her wig.

Emma lay beside her on the floor bleeding from the shoulder.

"Emma?"

Yeah right. It was probably fake blood. Daphne touched the wound, causing Emma to wince. The flesh was torn. Real blood poured out.

"They friggin' shot me," Emma cried. "God, Daphne. Get me out of here. They're going to kill me!"

"This isn't happening," Daphne muttered as shots continued to fire and screams exploded throughout the room. Daphne inspected Emma's wound again, unable to believe it was real. As Daphne reached out to touch the blood pooling on the marble floor, her hand shook uncontrollably. Some of the blood got on the lacy sleeve of Daphne's dress. "Why would they do this? Do you think it was an accident?"

More firing. Daphne flattened beside Emma.

"They must have heard me talking to you." Emma gasped like a fish out of water. "They're going to kill me, I know it."

"They're not going to kill you."

They wouldn't. Dr. Gray wouldn't risk losing her precious Purgatorium. But Daphne wondered just how far the Mad Hatter would go.

CHAPTER TEN

Helicopter Hostages

Daphne folded her hands across the back of her wig and screamed, "You shot Emma! You shot her for real!" She had to believe Emma was shot by accident; otherwise, the terror would be too much.

The tallest of the three shooters stepped toward her. "Of course, I shot her for real. You think this is a game?" He grabbed Daphne's wrist and pulled her to the center of the room. "You're coming with me."

She staggered, nearly tripping on the hem of her costume. As she adjusted her wig, she wondered if it was possible the shooters *weren't* part of an exercise. That seemed unlikely, especially since Pete had described a similar scenario. No, the odds of gunmen coming to the island to take over the ball were ridiculously small. Daphne searched the crowd. Everyone was on the ground. Brock, Cam, and Bridget stared up at her in horror. Her parents were perched on the floor, their faces peering at her from behind the bar. Dr. Gray was beside them, her eyes narrowed.

Daphne stared back at the doctor with wide eyes. Hortense Gray was mad, and all her minions were mad, too.

"Take me instead!" Brock shouted from where he lay on the floor.

"Shut up!" the tall gunman ordered.

"Shoot him!" another shouted.

"No!" Daphne pleaded. "Stop the game!" This *was* a game, right? They were just playing along.

A string of bullets grazed her boot, narrowly missing her toes. Daphne screamed and then clamped her mouth closed.

"Where's Arturo Gomez?" The shooter dragged her toward the doors where another stood with his gun pointed.

No one said anything.

"I'm going to kill this girl if someone doesn't tell me where he is."

Arturo, dressed as a jester, stood up. "I'm here."

Daphne was horrified to see that Arturo had wet himself. The front of his costume was soaked. No, he must have poured water on his lap. Yet, she hadn't seen him move since he hit the floor a few yards away from her. Did he do it on purpose? For the sake of the exercise? This was insane.

"We want the money from your safe and your helicopter out of here," the shooter demanded. "Who here can fly the bird?" He motioned to the roof with his gun.

Arturo looked around the room. Maybe he was looking for his pilot.

Daphne was shocked to see her father raise a shaky hand. "I'm a pilot. Take me."

Had Dr. Gray arranged this event to get her father to fly a helicopter? Tears of anger stung Daphne's eyes, and she glared at the doctor. Then she was shocked by a subtle smile crossing the doctor's face.

The shooter holding Daphne motioned to another to grab her father.

"Keys?" the man demanded.

Arturo Gomez reached into his pocket, shaking in a way that looked alarmingly real, and handed them over to the shooter standing closest to him. The man grabbed Arturo in a headlock.

"We're going for a little trip to your safe first," the man said, tossing the keys to the one holding Daphne, who must have been the leader.

The gunman led Arturo out of the room. The other shooters backed out of the ballroom with Daphne and her father. They were dragged into the elevator while Arturo was taken in another direction.

The elevator was saturated with the smells of sweat and body odor. Daphne thought she was going to pass out. Her father stood trembling beside her, staring at her with shock and fear. He was breathing rapidly, and though she was too, she was worried about his health.

"It's going to be okay," she whispered, though she wasn't so sure that was true.

"No talking," the leader said as the elevator doors opened.

As they emerged from the elevator and onto the roof, Daphne's father said, "That chopper's not meant to carry five."

"Kill the girl," the leader said, shoving Daphne into the arms of one of the other men. She looked into his eyes, hoping for a flicker of recognition, but she'd never seen the man before.

"Wait!" Joe cried. "I didn't mean that. I was trying to throw you off. The chopper will hold us."

"We don't need her anymore anyway," the leader said nonchalantly.

Daphne couldn't breathe. This was ridiculous. No way were these men going to kill her.

"Then you'll have to find another pilot," her father threatened.

"If you don't do what we say, we'll kill you, too," the leader said in a low growl.

"Fine by me," her father said.

The leader motioned the other to follow him. He opened the helicopter doors, and Daphne and her father were shoved inside the cockpit.

As her father took the pilot's seat, she was forced to sit with her knees pressed against her chest in a tight space on the floor at her father's feet. The gown of her costume bunched up around her legs, taking up most of the floorboard. The leader sat in the co-pilot's spot with his gun pointed at her father. The other gunman climbed onto one of the seats behind them, which were separated from the cockpit area.

She stared at the gunman, asking him with her eyes, *Is this a game?*

But he ignored her.

"Where are we going?" her father asked the leader.

"Just start her up. We're waiting on one of my men."

Her father's hands shook violently as he pushed buttons and moved gears. She hated that he was being forced to do this. It was hard enough for him to ride one of these things, but to fly one? She hoped and prayed he wouldn't crack.

Before long, the other shooter stepped out from the elevator onto the roof with a burlap bag in his hands. He ran to the back of the helicopter and climbed in.

"Lift her up," the leader ordered.

"I need coordinates. I can't just fly her blindly," her father protested.

The leader crammed the barrel of his machine gun against Daphne's cheek. "You better damn well do as I say, or…"

Daphne's heart raced. She wasn't feeling very confident that her father could fly this thing. The helicopter jerked upward a few feet off the ground and wobbled in the air. The gun shifted from her face.

"I need a direction," Joe said, as he struggled to gain control of the aircraft.

"Up," said the gunman.

Her father eased them into the air. She could see the rooftop of the main building moving away from them.

"Now what?" her father asked.

"Head west."

The helicopter tilted too far to the right. Daphne suddenly felt nauseated. Was it possible to get seasick in the air? They hadn't gotten very far when she heard gunshots.

"Dad?" she asked.

"Don't they know we're up here, too?" her father muttered. "Why in the hell are they shooting at us?"

Daphne gritted her teeth as she watched her father fighting to keep control of both himself and the helicopter. She didn't know what to say, so she sat there and prayed to God.

"Get us out of here!" the gunman demanded. "What are you waiting for?"

"She's not a fast flyer!" Joe said. "And we're a heavy load."

"Dump out the girl!" the leader said. "She's dead weight anyway."

Daphne wrapped her arms around one of her father's legs, beginning to believe this was not an exercise. No doctor—not even a mad one—would take such chances with so many lives.

"You drop her, and I'll run this chopper into the ground!" her father warned.

"Dad!" Daphne said. "I'm scared!"

A shot rang out. The helicopter jerked and dropped several feet. Daphne screamed.

"Do *not* land on the island!" the gunman said. "Take us out to sea, further west. I got a ship waiting."

Daphne's father looked down at her, as though trying to communicate something to her. She gazed back, wishing she could read his mind. Then he sucked in his lips and took the helicopter down.

"What the hell are you doing?" the gunman shouted. "I said take us to the sea. I'm gonna kill that girl if you don't…" The man looked wildly angry. He was losing control. "Do you hear me, man? I said take her into the sea!"

The gunman sought Daphne's eyes. "Tell him, girl! The sea is safer! There'll be a boat waiting for us. Don't let him run this bird into the ground!"

The gunman's face was white beneath the nylon. Sweat beaded on his skin. He glared at her, as though attempting to transmit a psychic message to her, just as she had tried to do earlier to him.

The helicopter jerked in all directions, throwing Daphne against the door, then against her father's leg, and then back against the control board. Her wig shifted. They were spinning, and so was her mind. The gunman was just an actor, and now he was terrified that her father was going to get them all killed. They had to land in the sea. That must be the plan.

"Take us to the sea, Dad!" she cried, about to throw up. "The sea!"

"Listen to me, man!" the gunman shouted fervently. "You're gonna get us all killed if you don't take us to the sea!"

He fought for the controls, but her father elbowed him in the side of the head, and the gunman fell back.

"The sea, Dad!" Daphne cried again.

She closed her eyes and tried not to be sick, holding onto her father. She thought of her mother and of Joey, and how hard this would be for them to lose two more loved ones. She prayed to God to help them. And poor Brock. She hoped he would meet someone new. When she could, she kissed her father's knee, but then the helicopter jerked up and back, and she hit her head hard on the door and bit her tongue. She felt herself losing consciousness and fought to open her eyes. Her father reached out and grabbed her, and before she knew what was happening, he'd opened the door and jumped out with her in his arms. Her wig flew off. They fell in the water, her back stinging against the surface. She winced as her father scooped her up and headed toward the beach.

Then she heard the crash of the helicopter and the enormous wail of the propellers against the earth and sea. She opened her eyes as her father splashed through the shallow water to see the chopper dancing and floundering like a giant dying octopus about fifty yards out. Sparks and flames flew up. Daphne couldn't see if the others made it out alive as her father reached the beach and headed toward the woods.

Several minutes into the woods, her father stopped to catch his breath. They sat on the ground gasping for air.

"Do you think they made it out okay?" she asked him. She cringed at the thought of what might have been actors killed in an exercise gone wrong.

"Hope not. Just glad you're alive."

"Why didn't you land farther out to sea, like he said?" she asked.

Her father shook his head. "They would have killed us, honey."

Daphne doubted that's how it would have played out. She imagined somehow Dr. Gray's staff would have "rescued" them, and they'd be back at the complex by nightfall.

"What do we do now?" She looked around. She knew these woods. They were east of the resort, not far from the naval tower.

"Hide."

"You think they'll come after us?"

"I don't want to take any chances. Do you?" Her father's heavy breathing hadn't let up. She had recovered, but he continued to gasp.

"I don't think they'd want anything to do with us now," she said. "Besides…" she started to tell him about the possibility that this whole event had been a game, but she stopped herself. If she admitted to her father that those gunmen were actors and that he might have killed one or more of them, how would he take it?

"Besides what?" he asked.

"Do you think that might have been another one of Dr. Gray's crazy exercises?"

He looked at her with horror. "Those weren't kids wearing white powder, Daph. Those were armed men."

"I know, but…"

"That idiot had his gun right up in your face." Her father struggled against the tears. "I thought I was going to lose you."

She threw her arms around him. He pressed his hands against her back and let the floodgates open. She held onto him, her own eyes welling.

Finally he added, "I couldn't bear to lose another child. I just couldn't bear it."

The memories of her attempts on her life flooded through her—the pills, the knives, the near-drowning at Central Valley—and made her shiver as tears poured down her cheeks. But before she could tell her father how sorry she was for everything, the sound of someone approaching made her hold her breath and freeze. Her father did the same, and they looked at one another, her anxiety mirrored in his face.

"What do we do?" she whispered.

He put his finger to his lips and pointed up. She lifted her face but didn't see anything but the canopy of the tree.

He took her hand and, slowly and quietly, helped her to her feet. Then he linked his hands together to make a boost. He wanted her to climb the tree?

Not having a better plan, she put her boot on his hands and allowed him to lift her into the branches. The fluffy white dress made it next to impossible for her to find her footing, but, scared for her father's life lest he get stuck below, she made it happen. She could feel him shaking the tree behind her as she made her way as far up into the branches as she could go. The approaching person sounded closer now, maybe directly below them. She held her breath and didn't move.

From the corner of her eye, she could see one of the men she had at first thought was in a bank robber's costume. He no longer had his gun or the nylon over his head. She wondered if he was just a lost actor looking for help or an actual threat to their lives.

Her father looked about to pounce on the man. Daphne bit her lip. The man below was shorter, but he was stronger than her father. She willed her father to stay put.

Joe looked up at her, as though sensing her anxiety. He frowned and sighed, apparently unsure of himself. The man below moved on, deeper into the woods, in the direction of Scorpion Anchorage. He walked like a man who knew where he was and where he was going. The thought of asking for his help, now that the exercise was ruined, crossed her mind. She opened her mouth, about to speak, but her father gave her a warning look, so she clamped her mouth shut.

They waited, still as statues, for many more minutes before her father whispered, "We need to get back to your mother. Those clowns might be headed there to do more harm."

"I doubt it."

"Do you want to take any chances?"

Daphne shook her head and then followed her father to the ground.

"We need to go west," he said as he looked up, searching for the sun. "We'll have to go back to the beach."

"I know where we are," Daphne said. "Follow me." She thought of leading him to the naval tower, but after realizing she had never learned whether the officers were affiliated with Dr. Gray, she decided to head toward the resort instead.

"Keep quiet," her father warned. "We saw one, but there may be two more out here somewhere."

As she gathered up the skirt of her gown and trudged on, she hoped her father was right, because the alternative—actors injured or dead because her father refused to land in the sea—was too much to bear.

But it wasn't her dad's fault. Hortense Gray couldn't predict how her patients would react in certain scenarios, and that's why things like horses and helicopters should never be used in her therapy. If any of those men were dead, it was the doctor's fault. Her father was innocent.

She led Joe through the woods back to the coastline. The bright sun nearly blinded her, and the difference in temperature was immediate. The hot sun covered her body like a heating blanket. Once her eyes adjusted, she could see the propellers of the helicopter sticking out of the sea, maybe a hundred yards from the bank. A seagull perched on it, like it was the most natural thing in the world. Miles away were a ton of boats. Had none of them seen the crash? Weren't any of them on their way to investigate?

Daphne wondered about the men again. One was alive, but what of the others? Had they submerged with the chopper?

She scrambled along the sand, keeping as far from the shore as possible. Over an hour must have passed before they came upon the huge, ancient oak tree where Brock had helped her realize how her feelings of helplessness had been replaced by feelings of blame and ownership for Kara's death.

Beneath the oak, he had told her, "Maybe one day you'll see how typical that was, fighting with your sister over a borrowed shirt, and how impossible it was to know it would set Joey off, if it even did."

"Wait a minute." She had searched his eyes. "Are you still saying it wasn't my fault, even after what I just said to you?"

"That's what I'm saying."

Daphne had become rather fond of this oak and wanted now, more than anything, to take a rest beneath it.

As if reading her mind, her father collapsed at the base of the tree.

"I need just a minute," he said.

"Me, too."

"Maybe we could slow down. Without water, we need to take it easy."

She nodded, feeling the heat on her scalp. The top of her head was sunburnt, and now that she was finally in the shade, she could feel it. She took the hem of her costume between her hands and tried to rip it, but the material didn't budge. Her father leaned over and helped her. Together, they tore a three-by-three-foot square of cloth, which she then tied like a bandana onto her head. The lace of the material scratched against her sensitive scalp, but she had to endure it to protect herself from a worse burn. The sun should be setting soon, but until then, it blazed down on her relentlessly.

"You haven't been this sunburned since the time we went to Santa Barbara," her dad said.

Images flashed through Daphne's mind. She and Kara played in the sand while Joey splashed water on them. This was long before he had ever said anything about spies.

"I have dreams of that all the time," Daphne said. "Kara sings to me."

Her dad's eyes widened. "Wow."

"What?"

"You said Kara's name. That's the first I've heard you say it since…"

"Really?"

"Really." Tears formed in his eyes.

"I guess it was too painful," she said.

"Maybe this doctor knows what she's doing."

Daphne kept her mouth shut to that comment.

"Listen, Daphne. I want to tell you again how sorry I am that I checked out on you. I should have been there for you. It was like all the air had been sucked out of my lungs. My family was falling apart, and I couldn't do anything to stop it. Like a chopper without fuel…that's how it felt. Like a goddam chopper dropping from the sky and me having no way to stop it."

"Is that what happened in the war?" she asked.

He nodded. "I lost a lot of men. We were leaking fuel. Could have been worse, I guess. But it doesn't matter now. What matters is how sorry I am, little girl."

"Dad, it's okay…"

"Your mom and I had just been discussing getting more help for Joey, that very night. That very night, we had agreed he needed a new doctor." He took a ragged breath. "If only we had acted sooner, your sister would be alive."

Daphne's heart twisted in her chest. Her father was outright sobbing before her very eyes, and she wasn't sure what to do. "It's okay. It wasn't your fault."

He gritted his teeth, fighting back the sobs, but the sobs won out, and he shuddered. Daphne moved closer to him.

"I love you, Daddy. I'm so sorry that happened. You're right to call it an accident. Things just happen. Shit just happens. We gotta move on."

He wiped his eyes. "Did my little girl just say 'shit'?"

The corners of her mouth tugged upward. "Yes, sorry."

He didn't scold her. She supposed under these circumstances he would let her get away with it. There were more important things on his mind.

They sat for a few more minutes, when they were startled by the sound of her name.

"Daphne?"

They both looked around. They could neither see nor hear anyone.

"Daphne, is that you?"

"Stan?" She could swear that's who it sounded like.

"Thank God you're alright!" he said.

"Where are you?" Daphne climbed to her feet.

"I'm at the complex. I have you on live stream and am using the speaker system."

"Speaker system?" her father stood now, too. They both stared up into the branches.

She'd forgotten about Prospero's surveillance cameras.

"Stay put," Stan said in a louder voice. "Help is on the way."

"What about the gunmen?" Joe asked.

"The police have been notified and are on their way to the island."

Daphne narrowed her eyes. "Stan, they weren't actually…"

"Listen, Daph," Stan said. "I know this is hard to believe, especially after all we've put you through, but these pirates have nothing to do with us. We had something else planned. Something similar, but not this. You have to believe me."

"That's impossible," she said, searching the branches for the camera. When she spotted it, she jumped into the tree and kicked it over and over with her boot until it dropped like a dead animal with a thump on the sand.

"Daphne?" Stan's voice came over the speaker. "Don't do this. Trust me, kiddo. You could languish out there. We need to find you and get you back to safety."

Daphne found the intercom and kicked it the same way she had the camera. Stan's voice cut in and out until the device went dead. The whole time, her father was shouting from the ground below.

"Are you crazy? What are you doing?"

She jumped from the tree and landed in front of her father. She ripped the silver bracelet from her wrist and tossed it on the ground. "We can't trust them. They orchestrated that whole incident with the supposed pirates." Daphne wasn't one hundred percent positive, but she was close enough.

"There's no way…"

"It's how they operate, here, Dad. You have no idea what kind of hell I've been through."

"Are you sure you're okay?" He took her by the shoulders and studied her face.

"We don't have time. We have to get out of here. Follow me."

CHAPTER ELEVEN

Relinquished

The Victorian-style dress made it difficult for Daphne to scale the bluffs along the coastline toward the resort, so she ripped the skirt. The remaining fabric fell just above her knees. Conscious of the possibility of surveillance cameras every step of the way, she encouraged her father to move quickly. Plus, the sun was setting, and soon they would be surrounded by darkness.

Once they had put a couple of miles between themselves and the ancient oak, Daphne wondered if they shouldn't hide until the middle of the night and then infiltrate the resort and rescue her mother and Brock—maybe even Cam—but when she mentioned this idea to her father, he didn't like it. He didn't want to chance getting lost in the dark. Daphne had a feeling he wasn't convinced that the helicopter incident had been an exercise. He didn't believe Dr. Gray would go to such lengths as to put their lives in danger. Even after Daphne described Giovanni's exercise at Christy Ranch and told her dad about the set up on the bird trail and the sunset cruise, he seemed unconvinced that the gunmen were actors. Daphne wanted to sneak in and rescue her mother and Brock, but her father wanted to confront the doctor.

It was dark when they came upon the road that curved along the canyon ridge, and they followed it down into the resort. At least they hadn't been picked up and led to some other crazy exercise. Maybe her dad really could demand to be taken off and they could be on their way home tomorrow. They hadn't gotten far down the hill when a group of people rushed toward them. As they neared, Daphne recognized members of the younger regulars in the moonlight—Dave, Vince, Stan, Bridget, and Cam.

Bridget threw her arms around Daphne. "We were worried sick."

"Why didn't you let us come and get you?" Stan asked.

"Roger and I searched everywhere," Cam said. "We just got back minutes before you."

"Do you know how much that equipment you destroyed costs?" Dave asked.

"Look, everybody back off," Daphne insisted. "We want to see Dr. Gray. Where's my mom and Brock?"

"They're with the doctor in the main building," Bridget replied.

"In the lobby," Cam added.

Daphne and her father walked briskly toward the main building.

"They're all beside themselves with worry." Bridget took Daphne's hand.

"So it was a legitimate threat?" Daphne's father confirmed. "Not some cockamamie exercise?"

"Absolutely, sir," Stan said. "The police have already been here and will likely want to have a word with the two of you tomorrow."

"Did they catch any of the gunmen?" her father asked.

"Their pirate ship was found, and two men arrested," Stan said. "But the gunmen are still at large on the island."

"Enough, Stan!" Daphne shouted. "I'm sick of this."

Cam squeezed her upper arm in a painful grip, causing her to shriek out loud. With his face inches from hers, he mouthed, "Please," with a look of desperation that made her words stick in her throat. Why was everyone so worried about breaking the illusion? What would happen? Before she could say more to him, three figures emerged from the main building and rushed out to greet them on the sidewalk. Her mother and Brock couldn't get to them fast enough.

"Thank God you're alright!" her mother cried, embracing Daphne first and then her father.

Brock said nothing, but as soon as her mother released her, Brock was all over Daphne. By the look in his eyes, he believed the gunmen had been real.

She and her father were led to the leather chairs in the lobby. Dr. Gray asked all the regulars to leave so that only Daphne, her parents, and Brock remained.

"The police are searching the island," Dr. Gray said. "I can't tell you enough how sorry I am that your lives were in danger."

"But…" Daphne started to speak and was cut off by Dr. Gray.

"Our physician and her assistant are upstairs now waiting to examine you," she said to Daphne's father. "Because of your previous heart palpitations, the physician wants to monitor you here over night."

"No," Daphne said. "He doesn't need to be hospitalized. We need to go home."

"When *can* we leave the island, Doctor?" Daphne's mother asked.

"The next boat arrives in three days," Dr. Gray replied. "Now, Mrs. Janus, why don't you return to your cabana and get a change of clothes for your husband? Brock, why don't you accompany her, since I'm sure she's still pretty shaken up? Daphne, I need you to be examined by the physician as well, though I doubt she'll need you to stay overnight. Perhaps after your mother and Brock return, they can wait for you down here in the lobby and then help you back to your room."

Her mother and Brock each kissed Daphne's cheek and did as the doctor asked, leaving Daphne and her father alone with Dr. Gray. As the trio made their way to the elevator, a war raged inside of Daphne. She wasn't sure what to do. Her father took very little stock in Daphne's opinion that the incident had been a set-up. And Cam had downright scared her to death about calling the doctor out. She wrestled with her inner self all the way up to the second floor and down the hall to the clinic.

When she was alone with Philip, who examined her cuts and bruises—including the gash Pete had given her on the back of her calf—she asked, "What happens to people who break the illusion?"

"Have you been taking your antibiotic?" he asked. "Your leg looks infected."

She rolled her eyes. "They get shot, don't they?"

"Don't be ridiculous." He examined one ear and then the other.

Daphne could smell his breath and could hear his heart beating as he leaned close to look into her nostrils. "That's what happened to Emma, isn't?"

The doctor glared at her and whispered, "Emma volunteered."

"What?" Daphne jerked her head back. "You're lying."

"Why don't you ask her yourself? She's just down the hall."

Daphne jumped from the examination table.

"But remember one thing." Philip grabbed her arm, startling her. "Dr. Gray's work here is more important than any one individual."

"Isn't she supposed to be helping people?" Daphne stared back into Philip's eyes, refusing to back down. She was angry and eager to get to the bottom of this.

"She does help people," he said. "She has an amazing track record, in fact. But some of us are willing to make sacrifices to contribute to the larger body of knowledge she's gathering in this experimental therapy. You'd be wise to remember that."

"When can I see Emma?" Daphne asked.

"Promise me you'll start taking your antibiotic, and you can see her now."

"I promise."

"And remember one more thing, Daphne," he said. "It's not why, but what."

Philip led her from the room and through the clinic reception and waiting areas down to a private room. Emma, hooked up to an IV, was sitting up in bed watching television and sipping from a straw when they entered.

"Hey," Daphne said with a smile.

Emma glanced at Philip before giving what Daphne thought was a forced grin. "Hey."

"I'll let you two catch up," Philip said. "I need to go check on your father."

Once Philip had left the room, Daphne asked, "My God, are you okay?"

Emma nodded.

Daphne narrowed her eyes. "What the hell really happened? Were you being punished?"

Emma glanced up at a corner of the ceiling at a camera and then laughed and said, "Of course not, silly. That was just another exercise."

She avoided Daphne's eyes, which made Daphne suspicious. Emma was lying to her. What else could Emma do, though, when cameras were pointing right at them?

She spent a few more minutes with Emma before Dr. Gray entered the room.

"Daphne, please follow me to my office," Hortense Gray said.

Once inside the chaotic room, Daphne sat on the green chenille chair with art at her feet while the doctor glared at her from behind her messy desk.

"I told you we had only one rule: Do not break the illusion."

"My father and I almost died."

"But you didn't."

"What about the supposed gunmen? Are they okay?"

"All safe. And none of your lives would have ever been in danger had your father cooperated with them."

"Don't blame this on my dad. You created the scenario. You can't predict how people will react."

Dr. Gray did something strange then. She smiled. It wasn't an uneasy or uncomfortable smile, either. She smiled with confidence, with pride, and with something like glee. "Oh, but I can. I wish it weren't true, but I certainly can and am rarely wrong."

Daphne frowned, tired of being manipulated. "There's no way you knew what my father would do."

"I knew he wouldn't give up without a fight. He wanted to save you at any cost. And let me tell you something, young lady. That exercise saved your father's life. You'll see. He has lived a pathetic existence ever since the death of your sister. He's been but a shell of a man. He even blames himself for your brother's condition. He must believe that he saved you from a real threat. If he ever discovered it was only a game…" she shook her head as tears—*real tears*—filled her eyes. "Suffice it to say that this opportunity to save you has been a major force in his restoration as a complete man."

Daphne gasped, suddenly confused. "But, but," she searched for something to say, something to feel. "We could have died."

"Your father was already dead," the doctor said. "And I just resurrected him."

Daphne stared at the ground. "But the other actors. They would risk their lives?"

"They believe in my methods. They want to help others. And doing so helps them to repair their own broken lives."

"But the helicopter. It's destroyed."

"Arturo has insurance. It's easily replaced."

Daphne's mouth gaped as she stared at the floor and searched for other objections.

"And so now I shall keep your father sedated and in recovery while your mother has her turn."

"What?" Daphne's head snapped up.

"Brock saved you from the sharks, your father saved you from the pirates, and now it's your mother's turn to be resurrected."

"How?"

"The experience will be more authentic for your mother if you don't know the details beforehand. But I promise you it will be the most thrilling game yet. And rest assured that when you leave this island, all four of you will be fully recovered individuals with a healthier relationship with each other."

After Daphne had showered and changed into fresh clothes and a fresh scarf, she curled up in a chair beside Brock and, recalling that cameras were in every unit, decided not to confide her confusions about the Purgatorium to him. She needed to wait until they were someplace private—though she doubted there was such a place on the island. Even though Cam had once told her the bathrooms were camera-free, she wasn't convinced that they were and took special measures to keep herself covered as best as she could when using them.

Just when she thought she'd had enough of Dr. Gray's insane exercises, she'd been convinced of their merit. There was no denying the fact that her family was healing and getting closer, like they were before Kara's death. Of course, Joey wasn't here, but she doubted he could ever be as close to them as he was before his mental disorder took over.

She didn't know what to think, and she wanted tonight to be as normal as possible. Curled beneath a blanket beside Brock in the one striped chair, she stared at the television, and despite the comfort of being in Brock's strong arms, the only thing on her mind was the next game. She wondered how her mother was supposed to save her life. She turned various scenarios over and over in her mind for a long time.

The next day, after breakfast, she and her mother went to visit her father while Brock swam laps. Daphne was alarmed by how groggy her father seemed.

"Are they giving you too much medication?" Daphne asked him.

"Relaxes me," he mumbled. "Keeps me from panic attacks."

Daphne gave her mother a worried look.

"I'm sure it's okay, honey," her mother said. "Your father could use a little rest after all you two went through."

Daphne didn't press further, not wanting to draw attention to herself from Dr. Gray, who was likely listening to them in her special surveillance room.

She and her mother sat with him for about an hour. They mostly talked among themselves—her father being too out of it to contribute much to their conversation. As they spoke, Daphne studied her father. She hadn't looked at him—really looked at him—in a long time. The deep wrinkles across his forehead and around his eyes reminded her that her parents were getting old. He looked broken. Daphne began to hope it was possible for Dr. Gray to fix him—to fix all of them.

Later that morning, Daphne was sunbathing by the pool with her mother, who was reading a book, and Brock, who had just finished swimming laps. She was exhausted and half-asleep, wanting to soak in the sun's healing warmth, when a shadow fell over her. She opened her eyes to see Gregory.

"Did I wake you?" he asked. "Sorry."

"I wasn't asleep." She sat up in the lounger and rubbed her eyes. "Just resting."

"I was hoping to talk you into some snorkeling."

"Now? I'm exhausted."

"Sounds fun," Brock said.

"You would love it," Greg said. "One of the most beautiful coral reefs in the world is only a short swim south of our beach."

"You should go, honey," Sharon said. "I want you to have fun."

After some persuasive cajoling, the three of them managed to convince Daphne to join Brock and Gregory. Sharon returned to reading her book while the others checked out their gear from the lobby of the main building—including a swim cap for Daphne (which she wouldn't swim without)—and then headed for the beach.

Daphne wondered, as they climbed the steps to the boardwalk, if Gregory was bored since Emma was stuck in the infirmary. That was the only explanation she could think of for this unexpected invitation—unless this was indeed the beginning of the next game.

The wind pressed against them as they descended toward the beach. Despite her anxiety over Greg's motives, Daphne never got tired of the magnificent view. The hill of yellow poppies to her left shimmered in the sunshine, and the bluffs to her right soared toward the sky. Way out in the distance, she could see maybe twenty boats, but there were only three people on the shore—no one she recognized—and two of them were sunning, while a third built a sandcastle.

During their walk, Brock had been telling her and Gregory about his summer job with the YMCA and how they were expecting him at the end of the week. As much as he was enjoying the island, he needed to get home soon. Greg repeated what the doctor had already said—the next boat would come in three days.

The water was cold but absolutely breathtaking the way it reflected the sunlight and lapped toward the shore in gentle peaks. Unlike the coastline to the north near Prisoners Harbor and Pelican Bay, this side of the island had very little seaweed or kelp and was smooth rather than rocky. Her feet sank into the silky sand of the ocean floor as they waded out.

"You see that smaller island over there?" Greg asked them, pointing. "That's Gull Island. The reef lies just between here and there, about halfway, not quite a mile out."

They put on their masks and swam toward Gull Island. Daphne was alarmed, when she scanned below the surface, by the sight of a barracuda floating, motionless, just a few yards away from them. It seemed unconcerned with them. She hoped it stayed that way.

The muddy bottom soon gave way to more and more colorful rocks and shells. About three-quarters of a mile out, the coral reef came into view. Tubular pops of color—orange, green, yellow, and rust—covered the ocean floor. Then an enormous, bright pink formation, resembling cauliflower, shimmered in the light of the sun, where tiny orange fish circled this way and that. Beyond the magnificent pink structure was a collection of lily-pad shaped colonies, multi-color, like something you would see at the end of a kaleidoscope. Greg stopped to tread water. She and Brock followed suit.

"Isn't it something?" he asked them.

"Amazing," Brock said.

"It's only about fifteen feet below us, so it's perfect for snorkeling," Greg added. "Ready to go down for a closer look?"

"Ready." Brock tucked in his knees and then executed a perfect surface dive before Daphne had even taken a breath.

Greg grabbed her arm. "Listen to me. I brought you out here for a reason. We need to talk."

Daphne stared back at him. She pulled out her mouthpiece. "About what?"

"Don't let my mother suck you in. She's got good intentions, but she's a control freak."

"You can say that again. Did Emma really volunteer to get shot?"

Greg shrugged. "She told Emma we couldn't be together unless she proved that she was committed to this project. So, yeah, Emma volunteered, in a way."

"Do you love Emma?"

"Yes. I want to marry her."

"How can you let your mother get away with that?" Daphne asked.

"Believe me. I've tried everything to get away from her. I only came back to the island this time to rescue Emma."

"Then why have you been going along?"

Brock surfaced. "What are you guys waiting for? It's spectacular!"

"Daphne can't get a proper seal on her mask," Greg said. "Here." He removed his mask and handed it over. "Use mine."

Daphne took off her perfectly good mask and exchanged with Greg.

"See you down below," Brock said before submerging again.

"My mom can't know what I'm up to." Greg moved closer. "There are few places we can talk privately. Can you meet me out on the beach tonight?"

"Why can't you tell me what you have to say now? I'm going to tell Brock anyway."

Greg looked toward the shore. "We're being watched. Bring Brock along if you want, but come after dark, when no one can see us."

She grabbed his arm. "What's this about?"

"I overheard my mom talking about the next exercise. You need to get your family off this island, but we need a plan." He popped in his mouthpiece and submerged.

CHAPTER TWELVE

Escape

That evening, after nightfall, Daphne went alone to her mother's cabana. Since her father hadn't believed Daphne when she had tried to warn him about Hortense Gray's insane tactics, Daphne thought her mother should hear firsthand what Gregory had to say. When she reached the front porch of her parents' unit, she heard voices. Her father was still in the infirmary, so who was talking to her mother?

Daphne snuck around the side of the cabana, where she had hidden the night that the ghosts had visited her parents. She peered in through the window. Sitting across from her mother in one of the upholstered chairs was Dr. Gray. Daphne couldn't hear what they were saying to one another, but she gasped when her mother leaned over the coffee table to sign a paper. Her mother was nodding and smiling. Daphne was tempted to walk in on them to see what was going on, but she couldn't get up the nerve. She waited in the dark until Hortense Gray left. Then Daphne knocked on her mother's door.

"Sweetheart!" her mother said as she opened the door. "Is everything okay?"

"Can I come inside?"

"Of course."

Daphne entered the room but didn't sit down. "Why was the doctor here?"

"Oh, I'm not supposed to say. It's a surprise."

"Mom, please."

Her mother made the motion of locking her mouth closed.

"Whatever. Brock and I want you to come for a walk with us on the beach tonight."

"What? No, honey. I'm tired. You two go on without me. I'm sure it will be a lot more romantic without me along."

"Please, Mama?" Daphne used her sweetest voice.

"Seriously?" Her mother smiled. "Well, alright. Let me get my flip-flops on."

They walked together to Brock's unit, and then all three of them headed for the beach. Daphne hoped Gregory would be waiting for them as planned.

Brock held Daphne's hand and took the lead up the steps toward the boardwalk. The moon glimmered on the dancing waves below, but the beach was in shadows. Even so, Daphne was sure she could make out Greg standing alone at the edge of the sea.

"That wind is chilly!" Sharon said as they made their way down the steps.

"Look how beautiful the sky is," Brock said. "You can see so many more stars out here than you can back home."

Once they were on the sand and walking toward Greg, Daphne said, "Mom, there's something you need to know. It's important."

"What, honey?"

"Listen to what Greg has to say."

Greg walked out to meet them, but when he got closer, he didn't look pleased. "You brought your mother, too?"

"I want her to know what's really going on," Daphne said.

"Didn't you think the three of you coming out at this time of night might look suspicious? I bet we won't be alone for long."

"Get to the point," Brock said. "Tell us why we need to get off the island."

"Someone tell me what's going on," Sharon said.

"My mother needs to be stopped," Greg explained. His face twisted into the frown of a frightened child. He stepped from foot to foot, smoothing the back of his hair down repeatedly in a way that made him look neurotic. Daphne wondered if it was excellent acting, or if he was about to have some kind of breakdown.

"I love my mom," Greg continued. "She's got good intentions. But a kid died here two years ago, and she won't stop. The power has gotten to her head. It's because of her father. You won't believe what he did to her. She did it to me, too. She thinks she's helping."

"A kid *died?*" Brock asked.

Greg nodded. "And now I'm scared for Daphne."

"What did your mother do to you, Gregory?" Sharon asked.

"There's no time for that now," he said.

"We have to get off this island, Mama," Daphne said. "Dad and I were almost killed in that helicopter, but not because of pirates. That was one of Dr. Gray's exercises."

"You can't be serious. A girl was shot!" Sharon shook her head with disbelief. "And you and your father could have been hurt or *killed!*"

"Emma volunteered," Greg said. "Manipulated into it by my mother."

Sharon shook her head again, like a dog throwing water off its fur. "How do we know this boy isn't just trying to get back at his mother for breaking things up with his girlfriend? Or how do we know *this* isn't the game?"

"This is not a game," Greg said. "Look, how can you believe me? I don't know the answer to that. But here's the thing: if I'm lying, what do you have to lose? Nothing. You're in a game either way. But if I'm telling the truth, and you can get off this island, well, I've just maybe saved Daphne's life. And yours, too, for that matter."

"What does your mom have planned?" Daphne asked, dreading the answer.

"She's going to make you the Lady of Shalott."

Daphne gawked. "What? How?"

"She's going to get you in a boat alone with your mom without gas or oars, so you'll drift who knows where, without food and water, until you are so weak you want to die. Then she plans on saving you. But how can she control a drifting boat out in the open sea? That's how the kid died two years ago. She wants to try the same exercise on you, but with a parent on board."

"She wouldn't," Sharon cried in disbelief.

"That couldn't happen," Daphne said with a new feeling of suspicion. Maybe Greg *was* luring them into a trap. "There are too many boats around this island. Any one of them could easily rescue a drifting boat."

"Between here and the mainland," Greg said. "But out to the west, there's no one for miles. Sure, it's possible they'll be spotted, but that's not what happened two years ago."

"What do you want us to do?" Brock asked.

"Take one of the jeeps and get the hell out."

"We can't leave without my father," Daphne said.

"I didn't expect you to," Greg said. "I'll drive a jeep up to the main building after you head over there. Then I'll distract my mom with an argument. That should be easy to do. While we're fighting, you help your dad to the jeep. I'll leave the keys in the ignition."

"Then what?" Brock asked.

"Follow the road to Prisoners Harbor," Greg said. "There are boats there all day long. Just flag someone down who can take you off first thing in the morning."

"But the cameras," Daphne said. "They're everywhere."

"That's why you need to go tonight," Greg said. "Just hide near the harbor and wait for the first boats to arrive. Just promise me you'll come back with the police or FBI or *someone* who can help me and Emma get out of here."

"Maybe you should come with us," Sharon said.

"I'm not leaving Emma, and she's in no condition to leave the infirmary."

Sharon sighed. "I don't know what to think, but I guess we should play it safe and go."

They left Greg alone on the beach and headed for the main building.

As Daphne was about to follow Brock back up the steps of the boardwalk, she stopped on the sand and turned to her mother.

"What did Hortense have you sign tonight? What's the surprise?"

Her mother frowned. "She needed my signature for a financial transaction. I authorized payment for a tour on a cruise ship that docks here in two days and ends in Galveston."

"How much?"

"Five thousand dollars."

"I hope we can get that money back." Daphne turned and followed Brock up the steps.

When they reached the top, Cam and Bridget were leaning against the railing and gazing out at the sea, probably sent by the doctor to snoop on Daphne. Never in a million years would Dapne have imagined having to lie to her best friend.

"Oh, hey guys," Cam said. "Enjoying the beach tonight?"

"The stars are magnificent," Brock said smoothly.

"Headed to bed?" Bridget asked.

Daphne and her mother exchanged glances. Her mother was a terrible actress. You could read the anxiety plain as day on her face.

"Probably," Daphne said. "We haven't decided."

"Catch you later, man," Brock said as he led Daphne past the other couple.

"Why don't you hang out with us?" Bridget protested. "Maybe ping pong?"

"Or billiards," Cam said.

"No, thanks." Daphne did not turn back. As hard as it was to blow off her best friend, she forced herself to keep walking. She was scared to death to leave him behind, but he was too brainwashed to cooperate with her, and he couldn't be trusted not to tell Dr. Gray.

As they took the wooden steps down to the resort, her mother asked, "Are we really going to do this?"

"How can you ask that?" Daphne said. "No, don't answer. Never mind." The last thing she needed was for Dr. Gray to overhear them.

Even though she had chastised her mother for doubting their plan, Daphne wasn't sure if they were doing the right thing, either. Being on the island had indeed saved her life. And maybe Daphne's father *had* been resurrected from the shell of the man he'd been ever since Kara's death. The ballroom and helicopter exercises might have been scary, but no one had been killed, and Daphne had to admit they had made her grateful to be alive. She also felt closer to her parents and to Brock.

There was the chance that Greg was setting them up for the next exercise, but, as he had said, if he were lying, well, they were going to get pulled into a game no matter what. If he were telling the truth, then they needed to get the heck out. Whatever the outcome, they were right to try to escape.

When they entered the main building, they found the lobby deserted. They went to the elevators, even though Daphne was in no mood to ride. The doors opened, and inside was Dr. Gray.

It was like she'd been waiting for them.

"Going up?" the doctor asked cheerfully.

Daphne nodded as the three of them stepped inside. Her throat tightened. She could barely breathe.

"And where are you headed, Doctor?" Sharon asked as the elevator doors closed and Daphne focused on her breathing exercises.

"I forgot something up in my office."

They crammed close to one another in the elevator. Daphne squeezed Brock's hand.

"You alright?" he whispered.

She nodded, but it was a lie.

"Are you recovered from yesterday's scare?" Hortense asked.

"Not quite." Daphne immediately regretted the bitterness in her voice, realizing that, like her mother, she wasn't the best actress. "But I'm getting there," she added.

"We're headed up to check on Joe," Sharon said. "Do you think he'll be released in the morning?"

"I'm sure," Hortense said. "He seems to be doing fine. I was just with him a moment ago."

The elevator doors opened and all four stepped out.

Sharon turned back to the doctor, who had been the last to exit the elevator. "You didn't tell Joe about the surprise, did you?"

"Of course not," Dr. Gray said stiffly. "Have you shared the news with anyone?"

"No."

The doctor stopped in front of her office door and inserted her key card. "Good night, then."

"Good night," the others said.

A receptionist greeted them in the infirmary as they passed her desk and walked down the hall. When they entered her father's room, Daphne was surprised to find the bed empty.

"We're in here," a woman's voice came from behind a cracked door.

Daphne glanced at her mother and Brock, worried that someone was doing harm to her father. She was relieved when Joe's face appeared from what she could now see was a bathroom. A woman, dressed as a nurse (who knew if she was a real nurse?), led her father to his bed.

"How are you doing, Joe?" Sharon pulled the covers back and helped him get settled.

"Fine," he said. "Just groggy."

"It's the medication," the woman said. "He received his last dose a few minutes ago. The doctor says he's fine to return to his cabana in the morning. We just want to keep an eye on him overnight."

Daphne knew their real motive for keeping him. They wanted him out of the picture for the next game, but that wasn't going to happen. Now, if only this supposed nurse would hurry up and leave so she and Brock and her mother could go on with their plan. Daphne had no idea how they were going to get past the receptionist, though. She hadn't really thought this plan through.

The nurse had already removed the IV and was putting the empty bag and tubing away when Gregory entered.

"I thought I might find you here," Greg said. "Just wanted to say goodnight before I go to see my mother."

"Goodnight," Daphne said.

"Goodnight," her mother and Brock added, glancing anxiously at Daphne.

They were all terrible actors.

The nurse gave Gregory a friendly smile as she exited the room. He followed her out.

Sharon made small talk with Joe, asking more about how he was feeling and if he was still upset over the pirate incident. He said he was fine and wouldn't mind going on the bird trail again.

"I sure enjoyed that," he said.

"That makes one of us," Sharon said.

"Oh, come on," Joe said. "Up until the bugs found you, you were enjoying it, too."

Brock kneeled down on the floor so that he was eye-level with Daphne's father. "Listen to me, Mr. Janus," he whispered. "We have to get off this island as soon as possible. Trust me, okay? Don't ask any questions. Just come with me and your family now."

Had Brock given Greg enough time to distract Hortense? Along with anxiety over the timing, regret filled Daphne's heart as she watched the peaceful expression that had once occupied her father's face transform into horror. He licked his parched lips, gave a subtle nod, and slowly got up onto his unsteady feet. Sharon found his shoes and slipped them on his feet. Then Brock half carried him across the room as Daphne opened the door. They had no plan except to make a run for it.

The receptionist behind the desk looked up at them. "What's going on here?"

"We decided to help Joe back to his room tonight," Sharon said.

"The doctor wants to keep him here," the receptionist objected.

Daphne opened the door to the hallway and they all four rushed out, with Brock dragging her father's feet. They reached the elevator and were relieved to find it empty, but when it opened on the bottom floor, Cam and Bridget were there waiting.

"What's going on?" Bridget asked.

"The doctor said we could take my dad back to his cabana," Daphne lied. "But he's still groggy, so Brock's helping him."

"Daph," Cam said. "He's not supposed to leave tonight. What are you doing? Please don't do what I think you're doing. I thought you understood."

"Back off, Cam," Brock said as he pushed past him.

They hurried out of the lobby and found the jeep parked outside. Daphne's mom climbed behind the wheel. Brock helped Joe into the backseat. As Daphne scooted onto the passenger's side beside her mother, the jeep roared to life. With Cam and Bridget shouting at them to stop and think about this, they drove up the hill toward the canyon ridge.

<u>CHAPTER THIRTEEN</u>

Run

"Which way do I go?" Sharon asked when they came to a three-way fork five minutes later.

"Straight," Daphne said. She knew the way to Prisoners Harbor. It was the direction they had taken for the kayak and bird trail excursions. "But go faster. We don't want Cam to catch up with us."

"Cam wouldn't do anything to hurt us, honey," her mother said.

"He's been brainwashed," Daphne said. "They've all been brainwashed."

As the road curved around the stables a few minutes later, a figure jumped in front of the jeep. Daphne screamed as her mother swerved to avoid hitting it. The jeep jerked and bounced from the road down a steep hill toward the stables. Daphne couldn't think. A scream was stuck in her throat. No air moved through her. They were heading straight for a tree.

"Stop!" Daphne shouted.

They jerked forward and back as her mom pumped on the brake, but the momentum was too much. The jeep hit the tree, and Daphne slammed against the dash, her forehead hitting the windshield so hard she bit her tongue before tumbling from the open jeep and landing on the ground. Her right arm and shoulder throbbed as she lay there for a moment, trying to move. She spat blood.

"Mama? Daddy?" She shouted as she tried to roll to her back. "Brock?" She flinched when sharp pains shot through her arm. Scared for her family and Brock, she rolled onto her knees and pulled herself up. The headlights shined through the night onto the stables. Her mother was slumped over the steering wheel. The backseat was empty, but someone was at her mother's side.

Daphne ran. "Mama!"

"Daphne?" came the voice of a boy. It wasn't Brock.

The person standing next to the driver's side of the jeep was Giovanni.

"What are you doing here?" Daphne cried, as she looked over her mother. "Mama?"

"I'm sorry. I'm so sorry. I didn't mean to cause an accident," Giovanni said. Tears filled his eyes.

Sharon lifted her head. A gash about an inch long cut through her forehead. "I'm okay. What about your dad?"

"Over here!" Brock said from the darkness.

Daphne stumbled toward his voice.

Giovanni followed with a flashlight. "I thought you were dead. I thought the bear killed you." His voice broke on his last words.

Daphne frowned. "It's going to be okay. We're going to get off this island."

"I'm sorry I ran," he said. "I couldn't think clearly. And when I went back for you, all I found was this." He lifted the flashlight.

"Shine it over there."

Brock appeared in the circle of light bent over the form of her father. Fear filled her heart. She ran to them. Giovanni followed with the light.

"Dad, are you okay?"

Her mother came up from behind. "Joe? Joe, what's wrong?"

"My leg," he said. "I think it's broken."

Brock helped her father up. "We've got to keep going. I'll help you."

Sharon hurried back over to the jeep but had no luck getting the engine to turn. "Looks like we'll have to continue on foot."

"But Prisoners Harbor is still a ways," Daphne said, unable to imagine Brock carrying her father's weight for that distance.

"What about the horses?" Brock said.

"No way," Giovanni said. "I don't trust them."

"Pearl was *trained* to run, Giovanni," Daphne said. "Scout and some of the others are pretty obedient."

"I'm not getting on a horse," her mother said.

"We better hide then," Brock said, "because I'm sure someone's bound to be coming for us any minute."

"Mama, we have no choice. You can do this. Come on. We gotta hurry."

"Turn off those headlights," Brock said as they passed the jeep.

Giovanni ran over and switched them off. The stables were flooded with darkness.

"Great, now we can't see," Daphne said.

"It's better than drawing attention to ourselves." Brock helped her father toward the stables.

A dozen horses stared at them from their stalls, and none of them had on saddles. Of course, they wouldn't, Daphne thought, and she had no idea how to put them on.

Brock sat her father down on a bale of hay and grabbed a saddle.

"Do you know what to do with that?" Sharon asked.

"I'll figure it out."

"Over here. This is Scout." Daphne tried to help, but her right arm was useless, and it hurt like crazy. "I think my arm's broken."

"Oh, honey!" Her mother examined it closely.

"Ow. Don't touch it."

"Look, maybe we can put your dad on a horse and the rest of us can walk," Giovanni suggested.

"That's not a bad idea," Joe said.

"It'll take us forever," Daphne complained. "At least a half hour."

"Actually that's *not* a bad idea," Brock said. "It'll take me too long to saddle up a horse for each of us. I'm not even sure I'm doing this right."

"Plus, we won't be as loud on foot," Giovanni added.

"Sshh. Listen," her mother said.

They were all quiet for a moment as they listened to the dark night. Among crickets and the snorts of horses, Daphne heard the unmistakable buzz of an engine.

"Someone's coming," Sharon said. "What do we do?"

"Maybe they won't notice the jeep," Daphne whispered.

"It *is* pretty far down the hill," her mother agreed.

They waited as the headlights flashed over the top of the stalls and the sound of the engine moved past. The thudding in her ears from her own heart made the low buzz difficult to hear, but when the lights were visible in the distance moving away from them, she sighed with relief.

"They'll come back this way when they don't find us at Prisoners Harbor," Brock said. "We need to hurry."

"We need to find a place to hide until morning," Daphne said. "Someplace close to the harbor."

"What's that sound?" Joe asked. "Listen."

The stables were alive with horse sounds, so it was difficult to hear the subtle snap of twigs near the stable door. Daphne froze when she heard it. Someone was out there.

They all glanced at each other with wide eyes. This was it. The gig was up.

Brock was the first one to step to the door and peer out. He squinted and stared for several seconds as they all held their breath. They heard the noise again, this time closer.

Brock turned back to them, his finger to his lips, and then returned his gaze to the path outside the door. Daphne nearly screamed when Brock swooped forward in a rush, but she was frozen in her shoes.

"It's the fox," Brock said, revealing Mini-me in his arms.

"Oh, no!" Daphne crossed the stables and wrapped her left hand around the small device at the end of the fox's tail.

The fox struggled against Brock's arms.

"Don't say anything," Daphne said. "It's a camera. Now they know where we are. We need to get out of here immediately. Giovanni, help."

With her right arm useless, all she could do was hold the tail as Giovanni pried apart the device. Once he finally got it off, he dropped it on the dirt and stomped on it repeatedly, like it was alive, and he wanted to kill it. Tears streamed from his eyes as he pounded his shoe against the device and the ground, over and over, spewing dust up in his face.

"Giovanni, that's good," Daphne said, alarmed. She touched his shoulder. "It's okay. We're going to get out of here."

Brock released Mini-me, who scrambled from the stables, and then he and Sharon helped Joe mount the horse. Joe winced as they worked to get him in the saddle. He cried out when Sharon slipped the foot of his broken leg into a stirrup.

"Take it out! Take it out!" Joe cried.

Sharon slipped the foot back out. "I'm sorry, Joe. I'm so sorry!"

He lay across Scout's crest and wrapped his arms around her neck as Brock tied a leader rope to the harness.

"I hope I'm doing this right," Brock said.

"Where are the reins?" Joe asked.

"There's no way I'm going to bridle her," Brock replied. "I haven't a clue how."

"Can we go now?" Daphne asked.

She clutched her arm as they inched their way out of the stables.

"Avoid the road," her mother said.

"But I don't know the way without the road," Daphne pointed out.

"We can follow it from down here." Brock held the crook of her good arm. "I don't want to risk being caught in the headlights."

The journey was made more difficult by the steep slope of the hill. They tottered, like limping soldiers, with Sharon and Giovanni on each side of the horse in case Joe lost his balance and fell. Daphne was more worried about her mother hiking in flip-flops than she was of her father falling from the horse. The rest of them had sneakers or boots, but her mother's feet had to be killing her.

It wasn't long before they heard the jeep retuning from Prisoners Harbor. They froze in their tracks and held their breath as it passed. They saw the jeep stop about a hundred yards away, near the stables.

"Run," Brock said.

They clambered as fast as they could, Daphne hugging her broken arm to her side but unable to stop the excruciating pain caused by its movement. Sweat beaded on her face, even though the night air was chilly. She wanted to throw up.

"We've got to get off this path," Joe said, still clinging to Scout's neck. "As soon as they find a horse missing, they'll know our plan."

"Cut to the right," Giovanni said. "We can hide in those trees. I've been there all day."

"No," Daphne said breathlessly. "That's the next place they'll look. They'll know you were there because of Mini-me."

"We can't stay near this road much longer," Joe said.

"If they expect us to take to the woods, then let's climb the hill and cross the road to the other side," Sharon said.

"We better do it now," Brock said.

Daphne gulped for air as Brock pulled her up the hill. She dry-heaved but kept climbing with her legs as fast as she could. Giovanni helped her mother, who struggled in her flimsy flip-flops. When they reached the road at the top of the hill, they darted across to the other side and half-tumbled back down again toward Central Valley, her father groaning with pain.

At the bottom, there was no time to stop to catch a breath. They ran on, parallel with the road until Daphne recognized the bluff looming before them in the moonlight.

"If we climb that, we'll be able to see Prisoners Harbor," she said. "It's about another half-mile on the other side."

"Honey, you can't climb that," her mother said. "Not with a broken arm. And I don't think I can climb it even *without* a broken arm."

"They won't look for us up there," Joe said. "That's for damn sure."

"It might not be as hard as it looks," Brock said, leading them toward it.

Of course, he wasn't wearing flip-flops.

"If it gets too hard for you, Mama, we'll just turn back, okay?"

Sharon nodded.

As embarrassed as Daphne was about her bald head, she pulled off her scarf and wrapped it around her neck. Her mother ran up behind her to help her tie it into a sling as they walked. Then Daphne eased the broken arm into the scarf. The relief was immediate.

"Don't let go," Daphne told her father when Brock led the horse up the base of the thirty-foot bluff. "Hang on." She hadn't been worried about him falling before, but this steep slope had her stomach in knots.

"You don't have to worry about that," Joe said.

Brock zig-zagged up the incline in a way that reminded Daphne of a McDonald's play-scape she used to climb as a child. She was glad Brock was in the lead and she didn't have to think, because it took all of her concentration to deal with the pain. Her mom climbed behind her, pushing Daphne up. Giovanni followed. Daphne hoped they weren't visible in the moonlight from the stables and surrounding area. If they could just reach the top, they could move out of sight of the search party below. Her left arm strained as she pulled. She gulped air, her heart beating out of control.

About half way to the top, Daphne stopped. She was exhausted and in the most agonizing pain and couldn't go on. Her good arm was now hurting her more than the broken one. She burst into tears.

"I shouldn't have thought I could do this," she said through a flurry of shuddering sobs. "God, this sucks!"

Brock called from above, "I have to keep going with the horse, Daph. I can't turn back. Come on. You can do it."

Sharon stayed beneath her, but Giovanni went around them.

"Keep going, Daphne. Don't stop," he said as he passed.

"It's okay, honey," Sharon said. "I'll stay here with you if you need a break. Just take in a nice deep breath and slow down your breathing. Come on, nice and deep and slow."

Daphne bit back her tears and tried to do as her mother had said. She looked down below, which was mostly in shadows. She could see part of the road, and although the stables were shrouded in darkness, she could make out two tiny pricks of light she knew were headlights. The jeep was coming back this way. She reached up with her good arm and pulled.

Her mother pushed from behind, and a few minutes later, Brock returned. He pulled on her good arm while her mother pushed her bottom, and together they helped her up the steep slope. When they reached the top, she collapsed on the ground and gasped for air. The sight of Prisoners Harbor filled her with unexpected joy. It looked farther away than she remembered, but the moonlit pier was unmistakable. If they could just get to it before the others discovered them.

Just then the buzz of a helicopter roared above from the east. It was coming to the island from the mainland. Arturo hadn't wasted any time in finding a replacement.

"Quick!" Brock said. "Take cover over here!"

He led them to a stack of boulders that shielded them from the chopper. They expected searchlights, but the helicopter changed direction and headed south toward the resort.

"Thank God," Joe muttered.

"Can we rest here for a minute?" Daphne sat on the ground with her back against the boulders. "I don't think they'll see us up here."

Joe was still slumped across the horse's crest with his arms wrapped around its neck. The others sat against the boulders, panting.

"I'm so sorry we sent you here." Sharon's voice cracked as she broke into tears. "We had no idea what we were getting into."

"Mama, please don't blame yourself. You couldn't have known."

"We were trying to save your life, not endanger it," Joe added.

"This place *has* saved my life," Daphne said, overcome by more tears. "You don't know this, but I came here to end it." She could barely watch the looks of horror that came over her parents and Brock, and she was no longer able to speak or breathe.

"Oh, Daphne," her mother held Daphne's good hand. "My sweet, little girl. Please tell me you don't feel that way anymore."

Daphne shook her head, still unable to speak. Two years of anger, hate, and guilt boiled in her throat. She coughed and wiped her eyes.

"I think the hardest part of life is accepting things we can't control," Brock said. "And when we can't, we look for someone else to blame."

"I did that to you, Daphne." Her mother's voice cracked with sobs. "And I'm so very sorry."

Daphne still couldn't speak. Her entire body shuddered as her throat constricted. A few seconds passed before she could finally suck in air and breathe.

Her mother sat beside her and put an arm around her, careful of the broken arm in the sling. "I love you so much, Daphne. I'm sorry we put you in danger, but I have to admit that I feel so relieved to have you back again." Sharon kissed Daphne's cheek.

Brock took Daphne's good hand and kissed it, and she felt a tear from his face land on her skin. Everyone was quiet except for the crying. The cold night air clung to them, and Daphne was comforted by the warmth of Brock and her mother on either side of her.

"Should we hide here until morning?" Giovanni asked after a while. "No use sitting on the dock all night only to be found by Dr. Gray before morning."

Brock squeezed Daphne's hand. "Let's take a break, but I don't think we should wait till morning. It's still a ways to the pier."

"Well, if we don't wait up here and we can't wait down there, what should we do?" Giovanni asked.

"I have a crazy idea," Daphne said. "And none of you will like it."

CHAPTER FOURTEEN

Hideout

According to Joe's wristwatch, midnight was approaching, which meant three hours had passed since Daphne and her mom and Brock had met Greg on the beach. As they crept across the mesa toward Prisoners Harbor, Daphne wondered how much more time it would take to reach the coastline.

The mesa where they had been resting stretched about fifty yards across before it dropped into a series of hills that descended in height all the way down to the harbor. Luckily, none of them were as steep as the bluff they had just climbed. They trudged across the hills in silence (they were all too tired to speak) for another twenty minutes before they finally reached the kayak hut.

"It's locked." Daphne was full of disappointment. Now what were they going to do?

"That's easy." Giovanni reached into his back pocket and pulled out his wallet. From there, he brought out the key card to his unit. He slid the card between the door and the door frame right near the knob. The door opened.

"How did you do that?" Sharon asked.

Giovanni grinned. "It only works on one kind of knob, but lucky for us, it's the most common kind."

Daphne found a switch and flipped on the lights. There were about two dozen kayaks, both single and double seaters, stacked along one wall of the hut. Another dozen or so life vests were piled in a corner.

They also found cases of bottled water and whistles. Brock put bottles in each of the pockets of his jeans and handed two more over to Giovanni and Joe, who did the same. Sharon helped Daphne and Joe into life vests before putting one on herself. Then Brock, Sharon, and Giovanni each grabbed a kayak and carried them down the path to the harbor while Daphne used her good arm to lead Scout.

Except for the sound of the ocean waves crashing against the rocky shoreline, the night was eerily quiet as Brock helped Joe into the back of his two-seater kayak and Daphne in the back of Sharon's. Even the pelicans, which squawked on this part of the island all day long, were quiet. The fox had been following the group from the stables, but now, as the humans eased into their kayaks and paddled away, both the fox and the horse, with ten yards between them, stood watching.

Daphne's mom had a hard time keeping up with the others, and Daphne felt sorry that she couldn't help paddle. She begged her mom to let her try, but Sharon wouldn't hear of it. The shallow water they maneuvered in was full of rocks, kelp, and seaweed, and Daphne was sure there was plenty of unseen wildlife below and around them. She could hear the occasional flutter of water as something moved away from their kayak.

"Talk about spooky," she whispered.

"We're going to be fine," her mother said.

But her mother sounded as frightened as Daphne.

"Twins Rock Cave should be up ahead," Daphne said.

At least a half hour passed before she could make out the massive twin columns guarding the entrance of the sea cave. Brock led the way inside. After having been trapped here for nearly four hours with Cam and the others, Daphne was nervous as her mother navigated them through the narrow opening. But this had, after all, been Daphne's idea. The cave would make the perfect hideout while they waited for morning.

Giovanni turned on the flashlight and illuminated the cave. The figures on the high back shelf glared down at them. Bottled water was passed around to each of them. Daphne couldn't open hers, which brought tears of frustration to her eyes. The exhaustion and helplessness overwhelmed her.

"Let me get that for you, honey." Her mom reached around in her seat and twisted off the cap.

"Thanks." Daphne gulped down the water in no time at all.

Then she closed her eyes and breathed in a slow, deep breath.

"Are you alright?" her mother asked.

"Yes, Mama," she lied. "What about you?"

"Glad to take a break. This was a great idea, Daph—though I know it's hard for you. We can all relax now. Who would ever think to look for us in here?"

"Hopefully no one will notice the missing kayaks and life jackets," Joe said.

"We left the place looking almost exactly as we found it," Brock said.

"They have cameras everywhere," Daphne said. "Maybe even in here. But I thought it was worth a shot."

"Why don't you try to get some rest?" Sharon asked. "We can take turns keeping watch."

"What's the use of keeping watch?' Joe asked. "If they find us here, we're trapped."

"Let's not think like that," Sharon scolded. "Let's think positive thoughts."

Although the images of being trapped and of the rock caving in on them threatened to overwhelm her, Daphne was glad for the opportunity to close her eyes. She focused on her deep breathing exercises and searched for her happy place. The rocking of the kayak and the sound of dripping water lulled her, like a mother rocking her baby to sleep.

"Are you sure she's asleep?"

Daphne had just been dreaming. She, Kara, and Joey had been playing in the sand on a beach somewhere. They were children—way before Joey had accidently electrocuted Grandpa. Way before any of the sickness had settled into Joey's brain. She kept her eyes closed, desperately wanting to go back to the dream. It had felt so real. In this twilight between wakefulness and sleep, she could still see Kara's sweet face smiling at her as she scooped sand into her pail.

Oh, Kara.

"I'm sure," her mother said. "She's completely out."

"What are we going to tell her?" her father asked.

"You can't tell her the truth," Brock said. "She'll never leave."

Daphne's eyes snapped open. What was going on?

"What have I done?" her mother said, breaking into tears.

"Daphne," Brock said. "You're awake."

"Why are you crying?" Daphne asked her mother. "What were you talking about?"

Daphne's throat constricted until she could barely breathe. Why weren't they answering her? Had her own family—had Brock—betrayed her?

"Answer me," she demanded.

She looked from face to face—except for her mother's, because her back was to Daphne—but none met her gaze.

"Giovanni." She craned her neck to see him floating in his kayak a few feet behind her. "Tell me what's going on."

He avoided her eyes. "You're lucky, Daphne."

"What's that supposed to mean?" She continued to search the faces of those she could see around her, but they averted them, making it hard for her to read their expressions. Plus, she couldn't see clearly in the dark, even with Giovanni's flashlight pointed up to the dome ceiling above and casting a glow on the entire cave.

"Your family loves you," he said.

"If they love me so much, why won't they tell me what's going on?"

Her mother patted Daphne's feet, which flanked her mother's hips. "There's nothing going on, sweetheart. I was telling your father that I regret sending you to this place. Cam's mother spoke so highly of it, and we trusted her."

Daphne studied Brock. "What truth can't you tell me?"

Brock stared back at her dumbly.

"I told him something I didn't want you to know," Sharon said. "I told him how we found out about this place."

"How did you?" Daphne asked.

Sharon told Daphne what she'd already guessed—that Cam's mother had recommended the therapy, and that she and Cam had come to talk to Sharon and Joe about it one day when Daphne wasn't at home.

"Why would that make me not want to leave?" Daphne asked.

Brock cleared his throat. "I thought if you knew, you wouldn't want to leave Cam behind."

They were lying to her. None of this made any sense. Her stomach cramped into a knot, like she might be sick.

"It's almost morning," Brock said. "The boats should be here soon. The tide is down, and we should be able to see the sunrise from here." He pointed to the mouth of the cave where a dim hint of the light to come outlined the opening.

"Did you get some rest?" her father asked. "How's your arm?"

"It hurts," she said. "What about your leg?"

"I can hardly feel it anymore. The cold water has numbed it."

"Oh, I bet the water would help your arm, honey," Sharon said.

"I'm wet enough." Her legs and bottom were soaked from the journey to the cave, when water splashed into the kayak.

"Do you hear that?" Giovanni asked.

Daphne listened. Gulls. Gulls were flying overhead. Day was breaking.

Her mother paddled the kayak closer to the mouth of the cave. "It's so peaceful. You'd never know this was a horrible place."

"It's not the place," Brock said. "It's the people."

"Not all of them," Daphne said, thinking of Cam and Emma and the other brainwashed regulars.

Then a new glimmer shone on the surface of the sea where it danced at the cave's entrance. Within minutes, the opening became a circle of light.

"Are you ready?" Brock asked, looking directly at her.

"For what?" she said, not sure anymore if he was really on her side.

He frowned. "Rescue, of course. What else?"

Good question, she thought to herself. She wanted to know the answer to it. Seriously—what else?

"Let's go," Joe said. "There are bound to be boats out in the harbor by now."

Anxiety and fear ripped through Daphne as her mother followed Brock and Giovanni out of the cave. She squinted against the sunshine, which wasn't yet bright in the sky but was still brighter than the cave had been. The twin columnar rocks towered above her. Off in the distance, the whites of a dozen sails and a handful of motorboats were still too far off for a rescue mission.

"What if we're seen by the others before the boats get closer?" Daphne asked. "Shouldn't we stay in the cave?"

"It's gonna take us a while to paddle against this current," Brock said, leading the way. "Let's hope we make it to the pier at Prisoners Harbor before we miss our chances."

Daphne scoured the coastline for Dr. Gray and her minions, but except for the pelicans squawking up ahead of them in the distance, the rocky shoreline was deserted.

"Why don't we paddle out to the boats?" Daphne asked.

She noticed her mother and father exchange glances, as if they were hiding something from her.

"The waves get rougher the farther you get from the island," Brock said.

"That's true," Joe agreed. "We'd likely capsize, and with your broken arm and my broken leg…" He didn't finish his sentence.

They stopped talking for a while as Brock, Giovanni, and Sharon paddled against the current in the rocky shallow waters of the coastline. Through the clear water, Daphne could see beds of kelp and tiny fish. Farther out, she spotted two porpoises leaping in turns. Three sea lions pulled themselves from the water and onto one of the larger rocks to sunbathe. Farther off, the boats moved toward them.

Sharon was falling behind the two other kayaks. Daphne wished she could help.

"You okay, Mama?"

"Yes, honey. Fine."

"What were you really talking about while I was asleep?" she asked.

Sharon didn't say anything at first but grunted as she pulled the paddle though the water. Then she said, "Let's just focus on getting to safety. We'll talk later."

Brock had been right: paddling against the current was taking them twice as long as it had taken them to get to the cave during the night. The sun was high in the east when they finally reached the harbor. Two catamarans were within earshot. Brock shouted for help, and the others joined him, waving their arms hysterically.

The captain of one of the boats noticed and waved. "You need help?"

"Yes!" they shouted, over and over.

Daphne was filled with glee.

"I'm docking over at the pier!" the captain instructed.

The paddlers quickened their pace. The boat reached the dock before they did. The kayakers had to go to the shore because the pier was too high to reach. When they landed on the beach, all but Joe climbed out. Brock lifted Joe in his arms, and together they all hobbled up the steps and across the pier.

Up on the hill was a jeep, and standing around it were several of the regulars, who headed their way. Daphne quickened her pace.

"This man's injured. Can you help me?" Brock asked the captain as they neared the boat.

The captain helped Brock bring Joe aboard as Daphne, her mother, and Giovanni followed.

"Please get us off this island," Daphne said. "As fast as you can."

Cam, Bridget, Stan, Vince, and Dave had reached the pier and were hastening toward them.

"Daphne," Sharon said as she took her daughter's good hand. "Please forgive me for what I'm about to do."

Sharon kissed Daphne's cheek and then stepped off the boat and back onto the pier.

"What?" Daphne cried. "Why aren't you coming with us?"

"We'll be right behind you," Sharon said.

"We?" Daphne wrinkled her brow, completely befuddled.

Brock moved beside her and kissed her softly on her lips.

"I'm staying, too," he said. "I'll keep your mother safe."

Brock jumped from the boat as the captain pulled away from the dock.

"But why? Why can't you come with us?" She looked over at the captain and the other people, who were staring at her like she was an alien from another planet.

"Are you part of the resort?" Daphne demanded. "Is this another exercise?"

"No, Daphne," her father said from the bench where he was sitting, his back propped against the side of the boat.

"I'm sorry. I don't know what you're talking about," the captain said. "But I need to get my sunrise tour back to the mainland so I can pick up the next group."

The catamaran picked up speed as the captain drove them away from the island.

"Wait! I'm not leaving them," Daphne said, even as the distance between the boat and the pier grew to fifty yards.

"We have no choice," her father said.

"Why?" Daphne gawked. "I don't understand." She glanced back at Brock and her mother, who were surrounded now by the regulars. They all became smaller and smaller as the catamaran neared the edge of the harbor.

The helicopter they'd seen during the night rose up from the island and flew toward California.

"You see that chopper?" her father said.

"Yes. So?"

"That's Dr. Gray. She's on her way to get your brother."

"What?" Daphne's heart skipped a beat. "Dad, what are you talking about?"

"That paper your mother signed," he said. "It wasn't for a cruise. Your mother didn't know then what we know now. She signed Joey over to Dr. Gray's care. He's being transferred to the facility on the island. She didn't tell me until this morning, while you were asleep. She was afraid we wouldn't leave."

Daphne looked up at the helicopter, trying to process what her father had just said. Hortense Gray was bringing her brother to the island. For what? So she could torture him, too? Did she expect to "cure" him the same way she had "cured" Daphne?

"Dad!" Daphne cried. "What do we do?"

"We're going to get the police," he replied. "You and I have to go back for help. Plus, we're useless to them right now."

"But by then it might be too late." Daphne looked back at the island as the boat reached the edge of the harbor, about to breach the open sea.

"Don't say that."

Daphne looked down at her poor father, who must be terrified about leaving her mother and brother behind, unable to help because of his broken leg. He would stay if he could. She was only making him feel worse.

"I'm sorry." She walked over to him and kissed the top of his head. "Please don't worry. I'll make sure they're safe."

Then, without thinking twice about it, she climbed up on his bench, stepped over the edge, and flung herself into the sea.

CHAPTER FIFTEEN

Lost

Daphne floundered in the cold water, held aloft by the life vest. The waves were more turbulent out here on the edge of the harbor than she had anticipated, and at times, when she was at the bottom of a large swell, the boat was out of sight. Then the swell lifted her high, and the boat came into view long enough for her to see people pointing at her. The swells were such an unexpected threat, that Daphne's eyes strained with terror as she floundered with indecision. Should she take the buoy the captain had thrown out to her and go back with her father?

In those few moments of indecision, she lost sight of the buoy. The choice had been made for her. She would return to the island. It felt like the right thing to do, anyway. She had to save her brother.

Voices called to her, Giovanni's and her father's among them. She ignored them, scrambled out of the vest, grabbed a big gulp of air, and submerged as far under water as she could.

When she ran out of air, she resurfaced, took another breath quickly, and submerged, hoping to avoid being spotted by the people aboard the catamaran. Her mother and Brock didn't know what Daphne knew about Dr. Gray's techniques—about the surveillance room, the real bullets, the one rule that couldn't be broken, and the pretend ghosts on the west side of the island. Daphne had to stay and keep her mother and Brock from being manipulated by Prospero and her Calibans. She had to protect Joey.

Even Gregory had been afraid of his mother.

Without a mask, she couldn't see how deep the water was, nor could she tell if she was going in the right direction. She popped back up for air and looked around. The waves were high, and she could not see over them long enough to get her bearings. The morning sun was her only compass. She took another breath and went under, swimming away from the sun to the west.

The cold water numbed the soreness deep in her broken arm, but, in spite of that relief, she was running out of breath. She popped back up to the surface and rolled onto her back, sucking in air as best she could when the waves weren't throwing more water into her mouth and gagging her. She tried to ignore the thoughts of sharks and other sea creatures circling beneath her in water that could be quite deep—a scary deep. She shuddered at the image forming in her mind of her small body floating hundreds of feet above teeming predators. She'd seen Humpback whales out this way. One could be near her now! Tears pricked her eyes, and she clambered beneath the surface to take a look.

The blare of a horn brought her back to the surface, but she still couldn't see over the swells. A part of her wanted to swim toward what might be the coastguard looking for her, but another part of her believed she was the only one who could save her mother, Brock, and Joey. She gulped in air and submerged and searched for signs of the island. Spotting a rock underwater, she swam toward it. Although she was disappointed to find it was just a lone rock, she did get a glimpse of the ocean floor. She estimated the depth to be about twelve to fifteen feet, and this was comforting to her. She popped back up to the surface for air.

When she reached the crest of a huge swell, she saw the island. Joy burst through her as she recognized Mount Diablo reaching up toward the now blaring sun. But the island was east of her. This meant the current was flowing in the opposite direction out here than it had near the shoreline and had made her overshoot her target. So she changed course, swimming toward the sun, glad to have her bearings.

She heard another horn but this time gave no thought to swimming toward it. From the crest of the waves, she could see the island. Still too far west of it, if she didn't make better progress, she might drift south of it and miss it altogether. She scrambled, in full-blown panic, huffing and puffing along the surface in a one-arm free-style.

Dear God, she begged. *Get me on that island, please!*

How ironic, she thought. One minute she's praying to get off the island, and the next she's praying to get back on it. As she floundered through the water, she looked below her and was shocked at the sight of a barracuda floating quite still just a few feet below her. She thrashed against the water and backed away from it as fast as she could, keeping her eyes on the silver beast with its ugly under-bite full of teeth.

Before she had gotten very far, her back hit up against something hard. At first, she thought she'd been hit by a boat. She flailed and floundered, scraping herself as she turned to see what had hit her. Then the current bashed her against what she now realized was solid rock. The skin on her knee and one good elbow stung as she tried to push against the huge rock in front of her. But the current pushed her ruthlessly into it, and she tumbled over it, and now headfirst, directly into another one, knocking her out cold.

Her face and scalp burned. Her skin hurt all over. She was both cold and hot. Kara had just been singing to her, but when she opened her eyes, Daphne was alone.

She scrambled to her knees. She was on a hot, dry rock surrounded by water. She had no idea how long she'd been out, but the tide was down, and the sun was high—maybe at high noon. More rocks towered above her. She hoped beyond hope that she had reached the island and that she would find it on the other side of these rocks. Now, if she could only muster the energy to go on.

The sound of a helicopter somewhere above perked her up. She couldn't see it, but the sound made her think of Joey. She dipped back into knee-deep water, found her footing on the rocks, and climbed her way to dry land.

She gritted her teeth as the pain in her arm returned now that it was no longer numb from the cold water. Along with that pain was her stinging skin, burned by the sun and scraped by the rocks. The worst, though, was her unprotected head, which throbbed and was tender to the touch, especially on the left side above her eye, where it must have hit the rock. And although her clothes were dry, her sneakers squished beneath her as she climbed, and they rubbed unrelentingly against the backs of her heels.

A group of gulls appeared above her, and their song lifted her spirits as she climbed the rocks toward the top. With only one arm, it was slow going. Her driving force was Joey. She couldn't let Hortense Gray abuse her brother. He was too vulnerable, too weak. He wouldn't be able to take the harsh fear tactics of the doctor's experimental therapy. Hell, Daphne couldn't take it. She was so tired that she began to cry tears of self-pity. No one should have to go through the hell she'd endured.

When she finally reached the top, she found herself in unfamiliar territory. The rocks gave way to high grass. Hoping this was indeed the right island, she trudged on.

Her stomach growled and her dry mouth and throat longed for fresh water, but soon she was cheered by a sign that read, "Fraser's Point." Although she still wasn't sure it was the right island, the sign filled her with hope. That hope was further kindled when she came upon a trail that cut through the high grass. She followed it. About thirty minutes later she came upon a picnic table beneath a scraggily tree. The shade wasn't much, but it was something. She practically fell onto the table and lay down on her good side wanting nothing more than a drink of fresh water. A pillow and soft bed would be nice, but she'd settle for a drink. Even a sip.

As she lay there, she wondered what the heck she had done, leaping off a boat in the high sea. She had only been thinking of the ones she loved and of her urgent need to save them. She hadn't thought of the possibility that she might drown, or get eaten by sharks, or get bashed into rocks, or miss the island completely. She had wanted to save her family.

Right then and there, she prayed with all her might that she was on the right island and that all the pain and terror she had just experienced hadn't been in vain.

She might have fallen asleep, lying there in the shade (with the cool breeze offering some relief to her poor skin), had anxiety for her father and what he must be going through not jerked her up from the table. How could she lie here and rest when he was probably terrified that he had lost another child? She staggered off the table and trudged onward.

As she walked, she fought to ignore the chafing between her thighs and the rubbing against the backs of her heels and the overwhelming thirst. Although she could block those things from her mind for short periods, she could not stop thinking about her parents and Brock and Joey. She wished she could get messages to them. She'd tell her father she was alive, and she'd tell the others to trust nothing that came from the mouth of Dr. Hortense Gray. She had to get to her mom and Brock and Joey and then help them all to get away from this hell as soon as possible.

After at least another hour of baking in the sun, Daphne came upon a sign that read, "Black Point." But it was the sign beneath it that made her jump for joy: "Christy Ranch, One mile."

She wanted to kiss the ground. Instead, she half-skipped toward Christy Ranch.

The extra skip in her step didn't last long. A mile was a long way with no protection from the sun, a broken arm, open cuts and bruises, squishy shoes, heel blisters, and chafing between the thighs. By the time the farmhouse came into view, she felt like one of the walking dead.

CHAPTER SIXTEEN

Awakened

Daphne tried the front door of the farmhouse and found it unlocked. Her heart pounded against her tired ribs as she pushed the door open. She reminded herself that she wanted to be found—had to be in order to save the others. As soon as she stepped inside, Marty noticed her from where he was sitting on the sofa watching the large monitor.

"Young lady!" he cried, leaping to his feet. "My goodness!"

"Water," she said through parched lips.

He scrambled to the refrigerator and brought her a cold plastic bottle of water, opening it for her and lifting it to her lips.

She drank it ravenously, enjoying the sensation on her dry throat. He helped her to a chair at the table and brought her more food and water, all the while asking her what had happened to her.

"Oh, my goodness! You're on fire," he cried after putting his hand to her forehead. He set to work bringing out food, and then he laid a cold, wet rag over her scalp.

She couldn't speak. All she wanted was water and grapes and a bit of bread. As she ate and drank at the kitchen table, Marty left her alone for a few minutes.

When he returned, he laid a gentle hand on her shoulder, and said, "I have something that will make you feel better."

Before she could do anything about it, he plunged a needle and syringe into the side of her broken arm. She gawked at him and, within seconds, felt woozy. She closed her eyes and collapsed.

Kara had just been singing to her as Daphne blinked her eyes against the bright lights. In a few moments, she recognized the room of the infirmary where her father had been the night they'd made their escape. An IV was attached to her left hand, which was peeling from her sunburn. In fact, her entire left arm was covered in tiny flakes of dead skin, except for places where dark scabs covered her flesh. They itched to be scratched, but her right arm was in a cast, and only her fingers were visible. She tried to wriggle them. It hurt, but she could move them. With her left hand, she lifted the sheet to find she was wearing a clean hospital gown. She wondered how long she'd been out. At least a few days, from the look of things.

She lifted her good hand to her head, which itched like crazy, and was surprised to feel soft, thick hair, at least a quarter inch long, covering her head. This alarmed her. She'd been out for more than a few days.

A snort across the room made her turn her head. Slumped on a couch against the wall, snoring, was Brock. The corners of her mouth spread wide as relief swept over her.

"Brock," she said, surprised by the crack in her own voice. "Brock, wake up."

He jerked awake and sat up. "Daphne. My God, you're awake."

"Where's Mom and Joey? And have you heard from my dad at all?"

He crossed the room to her side and sat in a wooden chair next to the bed. "Everybody is okay. We're all fine."

She bent her brows. "Where are they?"

"Everyone's here."

"Even my dad?"

Brock nodded. "After the coastguard didn't find you, he sent the police as soon as he landed in Ventura."

"Has Dr. Gray been arrested then?" Hope spread across her face.

"No." Brock frowned, and so did she. "The police didn't find anything."

Daphne sat all the way up in the bed. Pain rushed to her forehead. "What? Didn't you and my mom…"

"It's complicated."

"I'm listening. And I don't care about the cameras. I want to know every detail."

"We thought you weren't going to make it." The corners of his mouth twitched downward. "The infection in your leg got to your heart. It's a miracle you're alive." He leaned over and gently touched his lips to hers.

At that moment, the door to the room opened and Dr. Hortense Gray entered. "Hello, Daphne. How are you feeling?"

"I want to know what's going on. Where's my family?"

"Brock, would you leave us, please?"

Daphne glared at her. "No. Brock stays."

Daphne couldn't believe it when Brock kissed her on the cheek and said, "I'll be waiting right outside that door."

Heat flamed through Daphne's body as Brock left the room. "What's going on? Where's my family?"

"You were quite ill." The doctor crossed her arms at her chest and looked down at Daphne, not with kindness, exactly, but not with malice, either. "When Marty brought you in, you were running a fever of 105 degrees. A bacterial infection had developed in your leg and had spread throughout your blood system. You should have taken your medicine. It was prescribed for a reason."

"I don't need a lecture from you," Daphne said. "What you're doing here is…"

"Saving lives," the doctor said calmly. "Including yours."

"We nearly died out there," Daphne demanded. "I almost drowned."

"I didn't push you off the boat. I didn't make you and your family attempt to leave the island in the middle of the night. You all did that on your own."

Daphne studied the doctor's face. "So you're admitting you don't control everything that goes on around here," Daphne said, testing her.

"Oh, I control plenty," Hortense replied. "More than you know. However, in order for my therapy to work, I must leave some choices open to my patients. This allows for a degree of unpredictability. It keeps things alive. It keeps *people* alive."

"Not everyone." Daphne lay back on her pillow, exhausted.

Hortense Gray's face turned bright pink.

So Greg hadn't been lying about the kid who had died. If he had, Dr. Gray wouldn't look like a melting popsicle.

"I don't know what you've been told, but no doctor is able to save everyone," Hortense said, recovering. She uncrossed her arms and placed her hands on her hips. "We've been feeding you antibiotics through your IV for two weeks. I kept you asleep because I knew you would run, which would further endanger your life."

"You've endangered my life the whole time I've been here. Why would you care?"

"That's not true, Daphne."

"And you've kept me asleep for two whole weeks?"

"Are you saying you wouldn't have run?"

Daphne bit her lip. Of course, she would have run.

"Your infection has been eradicated, which is why you've been allowed to awaken. But you should stay here until you're able to eat solid food and use the restroom on your own, just to be sure your systems are back to normal and there are no further complications from your treatment."

"I want to see my family," Daphne insisted.

The doctor smiled. "I'm afraid that's impossible at the moment."

Daphne narrowed her eyes as her heart picked up speed. "Why?"

"Your parents and brother are in therapy together and have been for several days." The doctor folded her arms across her chest once more. "They are deep inside an elaborate exercise tailored specifically for Joey on another part of the island."

Daphne couldn't breathe. Her brother didn't have the strength for this kind of therapy. He was too weak-minded, too vulnerable. Didn't the doctor understand he was schizophrenic? And her father's leg couldn't be healed by now. How could he be involved in an exercise?

When she could finally speak, she said, "What have you done with them?"

The doctor's smile widened. "Your parents volunteered. I didn't force them into anything they didn't want to do."

Daphne's mouth gaped. What if Hortense had manipulated her parents the same way she had manipulated Emma? Had the doctor threatened to let Daphne die if her parents refused to cooperate?

"Your brother has made remarkable progress in the two weeks he's been here. And don't worry. Your family will be back on this side of the island by this time tomorrow, and they are as anxious as you for a reunion."

Daphne couldn't speak.

"There's someone else who's been anxious to see you," the doctor added. She opened the door, and in walked Cam. "I'll leave you two alone for a while so you can catch up." Dr. Gray left the room.

Daphne glared at Cam, finding no words to say to him as a million different thoughts mixed together in her head.

He sat on the chair beside her bed. "How do you feel, Daph?"

"Angry. Betrayed. Used. Abused."

"Your poor skin." He gently peeled away some of the flakes on her arm.

She wanted to stop him, but it felt too good.

"Come closer," she whispered.

He leaned over her—their faces inches apart.

"Greg told me the truth about this place," she whispered. "He wants off the island. Blink if you do, too."

Cam broke into a grin. "Whatever he told you was part of the exercise. He loves it here. We all do."

She frowned as she scrutinized his features for signs of duplicity. Was he acting for the cameras, or telling her the truth?

In a low voice, he said, "Not everyone who volunteers gets to stay, Daph. It's a privilege."

"But…"

"Do you realize I haven't wanted a hit in over a year? A year and two days, to be exact." He grinned again. "It's a frickin' miracle."

"If you're cured, why do you stay?" she whispered.

"To help others," he whispered back. "It gives me a high like nothing else."

"Look at me," she whispered. "Do I look helped? My skin's peeling off. I've got scabs all over my body. My arm's in a cast, for crying out loud. I nearly drowned out there. How can you call this help?"

He moved even closer, taking her left hand in his, careful of the IV port. Was he going to kiss her? He continued to peel away her dead skin. "Don't you remember that night in the bathroom?" Tears moistened his eyes. "If Dr. Gray hadn't realized what you were up to and sent someone to wake me up, God, Daph…"

Daphne swallowed against her tightened throat.

"That was a hell of a night," he continued.

"Don't you know what I've been through?" Daphne whispered. "Don't you know what my family and Brock and Giovanni and I just endured? Anyone of us could have died." Then she asked, "Where is Giovanni, anyway?"

Cam sat back in the chair. "Your dad took him to the police. They checked him in to a youth hostel in Ventura."

"A youth hostel?"

"Yeah. He called his foster parents. They spoke with Dr. Gray, who's trying to get him back, to finish his treatment."

"God, I hope not." Then her head jolted up. "They spoke to her by telephone?"

"I don't know," he said. "But Giovanni needs this place. He reminds me of me—of how I was when I first came here."

She groaned. "You're so brainwashed. You can't even see what's right before your eyes."

He peeled off a long sheet of her dead skin, and she practically cooed.

"You're the blind one," he said, "if you can't see what this place has already done for you and your family."

She closed her eyes, so tired. So exhausted.

"And you wouldn't believe Joey," Cam added. "He's like his old self, before the accident with your grandpa."

She opened her eyes and stared at Cam. "How is that possible?"

"Dr. Gray's a frickin' genius, that's how."

Just then, the door opened, and Brock walked in.

"Dr. Gray said I could come back in," he said.

Cam got up from the chair. "Of course. I'm sure you two have a lot to talk about." He crossed the room but stopped at the door. "I'll see you later, Daph."

As soon as Cam was gone, Daphne glared at Brock. "How could you let this happen to my family! How could you?"

CHAPTER SEVENTEEN

Footage

A nurse came in right behind Brock with a tray of food—chicken noodle soup, a roll, and chocolate pudding. Daphne's mouth watered at the sight of it, but once the nurse had left, Daphne demanded that Brock explain himself.

"You won't understand," he said.

"Nuh-uh," she said with a mouth full of roll. "You're not getting away with that. Talk."

"The catamaran circled back to tell us that you had jumped and that they'd called the coastguard," Brock said. "Then they took your dad and Giovanni to Ventura, where an ambulance met them and took them to a hospital."

"Thank God."

"Everyone searched the island and the surrounding sea for you. I went out with Captain Jim, and we covered the area south of the island. He seemed to think the current would take you there. The coastguard had several boats out, too. They found your life vest."

Daphne's bowl was still half full, but suddenly her stomach ached at the thought of what she'd put everyone through. Brock's face had paled with his story. She dropped her spoon on the tray and lay back on the bed.

"You should have told me about Joey," she said. "I never would have gotten on that boat."

Brock frowned. "That's exactly why I didn't. I don't know what your father was thinking."

"At least he told me the truth."

"It never crossed his mind you'd jump," Brock said.

"So, what happened with the police? Why didn't they shut this place down?"

"The only thing your parents cared about was finding you, and they needed all the help they could get—including Dr. Gray and her staff," Brock explained. "Then, once you showed up half dead, your parents wanted to do anything it took to save you. They didn't want to risk waiting until they could get you to the mainland. The police asked a few questions and left."

"So, if I hadn't jumped…"

"It wasn't your fault. We shouldn't have listened to Greg."

"You're saying Greg's warning wasn't part of the exercise?"

"Dr. Gray specifically said her son is rebelling against her and we shouldn't listen to him. He's just mad at her because she doesn't want him with Emma. None of this would have happened if we hadn't listened to him."

Had Brock been brainwashed, too? He sounded like he meant what he said. A lot could happen in two weeks. "Brock, wake up. Quit talking like this. You sound like one of the Calibans."

"One of the what?"

"That's my new name for the regulars," she said.

"I don't get it."

"Dr. Gray had me read *The Tempest*. Have you read it?"

He shook his head.

"She wanted me to see her like Prospero. That's this guy who frees a spirit from a tree, and in return gets use of the spirit's powers on the island, where Prospero and his daughter have landed after an attempt on their lives."

"Where do the Calibans come in?"

She peeled at the dead skin on her good arm as she explained Shakespeare's play. "The spirit had been trapped in the tree by a witch, and the witch had a son named Caliban. He tried to force himself on Prospero's daughter, so Prospero made him his slave."

"Are you saying the regulars are Dr. Gray's slaves?"

"Yeah. But instead of using the powers of a spirit to keep them here, she uses psychological manipulation."

"If you saw Joey, you might be speaking to a different tune," Brock said.

"You really think she's helped Joey?"

"I know it. I don't know if it's the new meds, or this beautiful island, or her therapy, or a combination, but he's much more relaxed than I've ever seen him."

Brock hadn't known Joey before the illness took him, so she couldn't ask if he seemed like his old self. Plus, she didn't want to get her hopes up too high. "I can't wait to see him."

"You will." He planted a soft kiss on her lips.

She smiled up at him. Pushing her now empty tray out of his way, he leaned in and took her in his arms.

"I must look awful," she whispered against his mouth.

"Beautiful," he whispered back. He ran his hand over her new hair growth. "Beautiful as ever."

"I want to go home," she said.

"It won't be long now." He stood up and gazed down at her. "I know you hate this place, but I can't. I'm too grateful to have you back."

She sighed but said nothing. Not knowing what to say, she allowed herself to be held by Brock. He climbed up beside her on the bed and lay beside her, cuddling her. He ran his fingers through her new hair growth, his fingernails brushing against her itchy scalp. It felt heavenly.

Daphne had nearly drifted off to sleep again, when Brock cleared his throat and said, "Listen, I'm starved. Mind if I go grab a bite to eat?"

"Of course not."

He kissed her once more and left the room.

He hadn't been gone long when Daphne got a crazy idea. Using the fingertips of her right hand, she pulled the IV port from her left, climbed from the bed, and peeked behind the door. No one was sitting at the reception desk, so she slipped across the waiting room and down the hall toward the office of Hortense Gray.

She knocked twice, and when no one answered, she tried the knob. It wasn't locked.

The lights were on and the chaos was as she remembered it—books, art, the loom, and the record player all crammed and scattered without order. A bunch of flowers—half of them wilted—spread out unevenly from a tumbler-turned-vase. It suddenly occurred to Daphne how ironic it was that the doctor's office was so out of control.

Daphne crossed the room to the surveillance room. When she opened the door, she was startled to see Lee Reynolds sitting behind his desk.

"Ah, I was expecting you," he said. "It's alright. Come in and have a seat." He pointed to the desk on the opposite side of the square room near the door to Mary Ellen's office.

Daphne was flabbergasted. "What do you mean you were expecting me?"

"Dr. Gray thought you might be coming by. She wanted to be here herself, but she's gone to the Mainland to see about Giovanni."

Daphne sat at Mary Ellen's desk and scoured over the monitors for some sign of her family. She spotted them walking along a trail she didn't recognize—her father on crutches with a cast on his lower leg. She was shocked by how good Joey looked. His usual buzz haircut had grown out, his dark hair nearly reaching his eyes, and his usually emotionless face seemed more relaxed. He was talking, but without the headphones, she couldn't hear what he was saying.

"Where are they? What are they doing?" She picked up the headphones on Mary Ellen's desk, anxious to put them on.

"They are headed to a little cabin on the southwest side of the island," Lee said. "I'll tell you all about it in a minute. There's something else Dr. Gray wanted me to show you—footage that was taken shortly after Joey arrived."

Dr. Reynolds motioned to her to put on the headphones. Then he pointed to the monitor closest to her. "Watch there."

The monitor went blank for a few seconds. Then Joey appeared. He was sitting at the same desk as Daphne. The camera came from the corner over Lee's desk. Daphne glanced above him and saw the camera was trained on her. Back on the monitor, Hortense's voice came over the headphones saying, "State your full name, please."

Joey looked like he had when Daphne had last seen him: expressionless face, pale skin, and empty eyes. "Joseph Christopher Janus."

"How old are you?" Hortense asked.

"Do you want that in light years or human years?" Joey asked.

"Human, please."

"Approximately thirteen billion, eight million, two-hundred thousand, five-hundred and sixty-two years old," he said with a stern face.

"How many years has it been since you were born to the Janus family?" Hortense asked.

"Are you referring to my most recent birth? Or the very first one?"

"Most recent."

Joey shook his head. "Are you with the CIA?"

"I am your new doctor, remember?"

"How do I know I can trust you? We're under surveillance, aren't we?" His eyes swept up to the camera.

He suddenly looked terrified.

"I told the last operative that I can't get involved." Joey stood up and waved his arms in the room. "This interview is over! This interview is over! Let me out of here!"

The monitor went blank.

Dr. Reynolds said, "That footage was taken his first day on the island. Now watch this next clip, taken five days later."

Dr. Gray and Joey returned to the screen, sitting in the same places they had been sitting in the previous interview. Joey had a tan, and his hair was slightly longer—reaching his eyes. They seemed less empty and more relaxed. Daphne's mouth dropped open. How was this possible?

Dr. Gray pointed to the very same monitor Daphne was looking at now. "Take a look, Joey. I'd like to know your opinion about this."

The camera zoomed in on the monitor, which showed Emma sitting across from Dr. Gray with a desk between them. It might have been the office next door—Daphne couldn't tell. Emma was crying.

"Tell me again how it happened, Emma," Dr. Gray's authoritative voice came over the headphones.

"Lisa had her Barbie's boots on the wrong feet," Emma said, sniffling.

"Remind me how old you were," Dr. Gray said.

"I was five. Lisa was four. Our mother was helping us cross the street to the bus stop. I don't know why it bothered me so much that the Barbie's boots were on the wrong feet, but it did, and it made me angry that Lisa wouldn't let me fix them."

"So, what happened?" Dr. Gray asked.

"While we were crossing the street, I reached behind my mom and grabbed the Barbie from Lisa. I grabbed her by the boot, and the Barbie fell in the street. We had just reached the bus stop when Lisa saw the Barbie and ran to get her." Emma broke down crying.

"Then what happened?" Dr. Gray asked.

"You know what happened!" Emma shouted. "Why do I have to say it?"

"Because it helps," Dr. Gray said. "Trust me and go on. What happened next?"

"The car hit her," Emma said, racked with sobs. "The car hit and killed Lisa, and it was my fault."

The camera returned to Joey, who sat emotionless behind Mary Ellen's desk.

"Do you see a similarity in Emma's experience to the one you had with your grandfather?"

"No," Joey said.

"No?" Dr. Gray echoed. "You can't see how what happened to Emma's sister cannot be blamed on Emma? She was a child. She was doing what children do. It was a tragic accident, just like what happened to your grandfather was an accident and not your fault."

"But the CIA told me to electrocute my grandfather," Joey explained. "They said he was a threat to national security. I was just doing my duty. That's quite different from what happened to that girl on the screen."

Daphne looked across the room at Dr. Reynolds, but he continued to watch the monitor, so she returned her eyes to it.

"Don't you see that your brain has created this elaborate defense mechanism to handle the guilt you feel over your grandfather's death? It's easier to believe that you were working for the CIA…"

"I *was* working for the CIA," Joey demanded. "My good friend Judge William Clark can verify that. Call him."

"Watch the screen, Joey," Dr. Gray said.

Daphne asked Dr. Reynolds, "Was Emma acting in that video?"

"No," Lee said. "That's what really happened to her sister."

The camera zoomed in on the monitor, and now Kelly, the horse guide, sat behind the desk from Hortense.

"Tell me again what happened the night your son died," Hortense said.

"Do I really have to go through this with you again?" Kelly complained.

"Yes, please. Once more. Two years ago…"

"We were all in bed asleep. I heard footsteps and realized Nathan had gone downstairs. I listened for him to return. I was about to go check on him, when I heard him climb back up to his room. I knew he had gone down for some water and was proud that he could finally do it all by himself."

"How old was he?" Dr. Gray asked.

"Three and a half," Kelly said with a frown. "My baby was three and a half years old."

"Go on," Dr. Gray said. "What happened next?"

"I had fallen asleep when I was startled awake by a noise. I heard it again but couldn't tell what it was. I thought maybe a tree was hitting the roof." Kelly broke into tears. "It was Nathan kicking the wall! I should have gotten up! If only I would have gotten out of bed and checked!"

Daphne grabbed her stomach, feeling sick and dizzy.

"You couldn't have known," Hortense said. "Please, tell me what happened next."

"I fell back asleep," Kelly said. "And in the morning, we found Nathan hanging between the slats of the top bunk. He had taken the ladder from his closet. We hadn't put a mattress on the top bunk. He had fallen through the slats to his neck and had been hanging there until he…We had told him not to play up there. Why didn't I put the ladder in the attic or somewhere he couldn't get to? Oh, God! My poor baby!" Kelly covered her mouth and the camera returned to Joey, whose usually expressionless face wore a frown.

"What do you think of that case?" Hortense asked him.

"It's sad," Joey said.

"It reminds me of what happened to your sister," Dr. Gray added.

"Except the CIA told me to kill the imposter inside of my sister," Joey said. "Kara wasn't supposed to die—just the imposter who had taken over her body." Joey's lips trembled. "It wasn't supposed to happen that way. The CIA had promised me that Kara wouldn't get hurt."

"It was a tragic accident," Dr. Gray said. "Caused by your untreated mental illness."

"That's what *all* the doctors say," he said.

"But here's another thing I want you to know," Hortense added. "You haven't been getting the right treatment in Houston."

"I haven't?"

"No, sir."

"I *knew* it."

"The schizophrenia was brought on by the post-traumatic stress disorder," Hortense explained. "You've been taking medication for schizophrenia, but you haven't received proper treatment for PTSD."

"Where does the CIA fit into this theory?" Joey asked.

"Your brain created the CIA in a desperate attempt to protect itself."

"That's bull. I've heard it before."

"With PTSD, your brain gets stuck in a highly intense fight-or-flight mode, brought on by fear. In the wake of a traumatic event, a PTSD victim can't break out of fight-or-flight properly. Your brain, in that intense state of arousal, sought an explanation, and it came up with a reasonable one: a group with power made you its puppet. That helped explain why things happened outside of your control. It was easier than accepting your own helplessness. The rest of your family suffers from the same syndrome."

"But they've never mentioned the CIA to me."

"No. They dealt with their illness in different ways. Your father and your sister attempted suicide."

Daphne's head snapped up. Was that true about her father?

"All the doctors tell me that the CIA never gave me orders, but you're the first one to explain why I might think they would."

"That's because no one attempted to treat the PTSD. And you wouldn't have been open to my suggestions if I hadn't shared these other stories with you, so you could see the similarities. Also, I've changed your medications so that you are more cognizant and less numb to your surroundings. You've also been on a gluten-free diet since your arrival. Have you noticed the change?"

"I think so."

"Remember the blood work I did on you on your first day here?"

Joey nodded. "I thought you were inserting a tracker."

"I tested your blood for food allergies. You're allergic to wheat. Did you know that?"

Joey shook his head.

"You feel better, don't you?"

"Yes, doctor. I really do."

The monitor went blank. Daphne looked across the room at Dr. Reynolds, who took off his headphones. She did the same.

"Was that true about my dad?" she asked the doctor.

"Yes. I'm sorry you had to hear about it like this."

"When?"

"I honestly don't know all the details."

"I don't believe you."

He sighed. "You have to remember that Kara's death compounded the PTSD he was already suffering from since the Gulf War."

"What did he do? And when?"

"He tried to overdose with a combination of pills. Your mother found him in time."

"When?"

"I believe it was on the one-year anniversary of Kara's death."

Daphne's lips trembled uncontrollably. That must have been so hard on her poor mother. Her father in April, and then, on New Year's Eve of the same year, Daphne. How had her mother held it together?

"So, what's happening to my family now?" Daphne searched the monitors for signs of them.

"There's still one more tape Dr. Gray wants you to see before I explain what's about to happen tonight. Take a look."

Daphne turned to the screen closest to her once more and watched with the headphones back on her head. She was surprised to see Joey on a small aluminum boat with her parents. They were tied to the pier at

Willows Anchorage, where Captain Jim had met them in his catamaran for the sunset cruise. They each had a rod and reel in their hands.

"They went fishing together?" Daphne asked Dr. Reynolds.

"Yep. Take a look."

"This isn't so bad, now is it, Sharon?" her dad said.

"No, it's not, but you promised I wouldn't have to touch a fish," her mother said smiling.

"What do you think, Joey?" her dad asked. "We used to have a rule that when you reached a certain age, you had to take off your own fish."

"Well, you already baited the hook for her and broke one rule," Joey said. "You may as well break another."

Daphne was surprised by how relaxed and easy-going her brother sounded. His face showed emotion, like it used to in the old days.

"Good point," Joe said.

"Isn't this a beautiful place?" Sharon asked. "You know I never liked the beach much—I don't like getting sand all over me and in my clothes, but the island and wildlife around here are amazing to look at. In fact, look over there." Sharon pointed to something out of the view of the camera.

"Where?" Joe asked.

Sharon stood up in the boat. "Right over there. See it? Ahh!" Just then, Sharon lost her balance and fell over the side of the boat.

"Mom?" Joey leaned over, searching for her.

"She's not wearing her life jacket, son. Can you help her?"

Daphne realized her mother's "fall" was part of an exercise because her father was a terrible actor, but Joey just might be new enough to the island to not suspect anything. With his life vest on, he leapt over the boat. The angle of the camera didn't allow a good view of what happened next because the boat was in the way, but soon Joey was helping their mother over the edge of the boat while their father held on to the dock to keep the boat from tipping over.

Once they were safe inside the boat, her mother—not much better at acting than her father—said, "You saved my life, Joey! My leg got caught in a bed of kelp and I couldn't swim. I panicked. Oh my God, Joey. What would I have done without you?"

Sharon hugged Joey as she cried real tears. The camera zoomed in on Joey's stunned face. His fingers trembled, but there was an unmistakable twinkle in his eyes, which were welling with tears. Daphne realized she, too, was crying, even though she knew it was all an act.

The screen went blank. Daphne wiped her eyes and removed the headphones. She was glad that Joey was able to play the hero, but not sure if she agreed with deceit and manipulation as a form of therapy. Was lying to him really a good way to help him?

"So, tell me what my family is doing now." She had to admit that in spite of her reservations she was surprised to see Dr. Gray's therapy working magic on her brother.

Dr. Reynolds removed the headphones, leaned back in his chair, and pointed to a screen closer to him. "You see that cabin?"

It was a small wooden structure that reminded her of the tiny cabins at a little resort in Colorado—just four walls, only big enough for bunkbeds and a table that converted into a third bed. She couldn't see the inside of this particular cabin, but she did see it was on a cement slab much larger than the cabin, creating a wrap-around patio cut into the side of a hill.

"Yeah, so?"

"Our crew just rebuilt that cabin. I don't know how many times we've rebuilt it. Dozens, I guess."

"Why do you have to keep rebuilding it?" Daphne felt uneasy.

"You remember that day you went on the trail ride with Kelly for the first time?"

"Yeah?"

"Remember the smoke you saw?"

"Yeah?"

"Well, that smoke was part of a regular exercise we run on the island at that cabin."

Daphne rubbed the pain in her forehead. "What do you mean? You don't set the cabin on fire."

"As a matter of fact, we do. We burn it to the ground."

CHAPTER EIGHTEEN

Restraint

Daphne found it hard to navigate in the cloudy night with no moon and stars to guide them. It was tricky enough to find her way around the island in the daytime with the sun for a compass, but this was nuts. Roger had driven her and Brock around the canyon ridge, through Central Valley, to the base of Sierra Blanca, to a fork in the road. The sign at the fork pointed right to Chumash Ruins/Christy Ranch and left to Sierra Blanca. Roger had told them to follow the trail up the mountain to the cabin. He refused to drive them farther or to give them flashlights because he was afraid they would ruin the exercise.

"Keep outta sight," he had warned them. "And don't intervene. You're watchers. You aren't to enter the game. Let Stan and the others handle it."

Daphne was grateful that he and Dr. Reynolds had allowed her to come, so she hadn't argued. But now, as she and Brock plowed carefully through the tall, itchy grass growing on either side of the trail in the near-pitch dark, she worried they'd never find the cabin in time.

"This is ridiculous," Brock complained. "What are we doing?"

"I'm afraid for my family," Daphne said.

"Roger sent us on a wild goose chase."

"He didn't want flashlights to ruin anything," she said.

"He should have guided us on foot."

A circle of light on the ground brought Daphne to a halt. "What's that?"

"A manhole?"

At that moment, Stan's head emerged with a light attached to his cap.

"Hey, guys," Stan said. "Come on in."

Daphne glanced at Brock and then back at Stan. She did *not* want to climb into the ground. "Where's the cabin?"

"It's up the mountain," Stan said. "You can get to it easier from down here. Come on, we don't have all night."

Stan's head disappeared, but the glow of his light illuminated the steel ladder leading down a circular tube about three feet in diameter.

"It's okay," Brock told her. "You can do this. If it gets to be too much for you, we can always come back up."

Brock descended first. Daphne's stomach was in knots, but if this was the way to help her family, she would do it. She climbed down the cold steel ladder about fifteen feet to the ground, where she landed on a smooth rock floor.

"What is this place?" she asked.

"It was built during World War Two," Stan explained. "It tunnels beneath the mountain all the way to Punta Arena. Follow me."

With weak knees, Daphne held tightly to Brock's hand and followed, even though a voice inside her head begged her not to. Stan led them through the three-foot-by-seven-foot tunnel at a gentle incline for about a hundred feet. Along the way, Daphne noticed hatch doors, like one would find on a submarine, lining the wall of the tunnel every ten yards or so. When she had asked where they led to, Stan had shrugged and had simply said they hadn't been used since the war.

Eventually they came to a larger chamber, which resembled the sur-veillance room adjacent to Dr. Gray's office. A grid of monitors hung on one wall. There were desks and chairs, two of which were occupied by Dave and Vince. Except for a small desk lamp, the only light in the room came from the monitors.

"How's it hanging?" Dave said chuckling.

"Hey," Brock greeted him.

Stan closed the hatch door they had just entered.

"Do you have to do that?" Daphne asked, feeling like she was suffocating.

"Sorry, kiddo," Stan said. "I really do."

"Why?" she asked. "There's no one out there."

"I'm not worried about people getting in," Stan said.

Daphne's heart picked up speed. "What, then?"

"We can't risk you ruining the exercise for Joey," Stan explained.

Daphne looked at the faces around her for some sign, some explanation, because Stan didn't make sense. "Are you saying I'm a prisoner?"

"Not exactly," Stan said.

"Geez. Calm down." Dave added with a giggle.

"Then what *are* you saying?" Brock demanded.

"Look," Stan said. "Dr. Gray knew you would try to find this place on your own if she didn't let you come out here, but she also knew you would enter the game if she didn't stop you."

"So she ordered us to keep you here until the exercise was over," Dave said.

"What?" Daphne shouted, near panic.

"But you can watch it all on the screen," Vince said.

"And we are literally right under the cabin," Stan added. "If anything goes wrong, the guys and I can easily intervene."

"How? Is there a secret entrance from down here?" Brock asked.

"Yeah, but don't expect directions to it," Dave said.

He and Vince chuckled.

"Look, kiddo," Stan said. "I promise no one will get hurt."

"You can't promise that!" Daphne cried. "It's impossible!"

"The fire is contained," Stan said. "There is nothing flammable around the cabin. We have a sprinkler system installed, which we control from down here."

The mention of sprinklers calmed Daphne down a bit and made her less terrified for her family. "Fires spread quickly," she said. "I'm just sayin'."

"We've done this, like, fifty times," Vince said.

"You get to see your big brother play the hero," Dave said.

"And if he doesn't?" Daphne asked, fearing the worst. "What if he runs for his life and leaves my parents behind?" His illness made him unpredictable. There was no way of knowing how he would react.

"He won't," Stan said.

Daphne wasn't so sure. She turned to Brock. "I'm scared."

Brock squeezed her good hand and kissed her forehead. "I've got your back," he whispered.

"This could really help Joey," Stan said. "Let's give it a chance to work."

Daphne glanced at the monitors behind Stan and saw her parents and Joey making s'mores on the patio outside of the cabin. A lantern added to the soft glow emanating from the fire pit, which her family sat around in lounging chairs. She couldn't hear what they were saying, but she could see by the smiles on their faces that they were happy.

Stan noticed where her gaze had gone. "Ready to sit down and listen?"

Daphne nodded and took a chair behind one of the desks where a set of headphones awaited her. Brock sat beside her, and Stan handed a set to him, too.

"Look. The clouds have moved on," her father said over the headphones. "You can see the stars again."

Joey brought a mostly burnt marshmallow on the end of a steel skewer up from the fire pit and then handed it over to their mom.

"You like them burnt, right?" he asked her.

He wasn't kidding. Their mom really did like them that way. Sharon smiled at him and took the marshmallow between two pieces of graham cracker. "Thanks, honey."

"My good friend, Judge William Clark, told me that the North Koreans could be invading any day," Joey said.

Daphne frowned. Joey sounded like his usual self. He always talked about his good friend Judge William Clark, but, as far as anyone knew, no such person existed.

"The CIA probably has something in place to deflect any attack," Joey said. "But, but, I don't think they'll be recruiting me anymore. Maybe they never recruited me. Right? Maybe they never recruited me."

"I don't think so," their mother said.

"I'm sorry, son," Joe added.

As Joey held the skewer over the flame to burn off the rest of the gooey marshmallow residue, he asked, "When do you think Daphne will wake up?"

Daphne's hand moved to her heart. She exchanged a glance with Brock, who winked at her.

"Dr. Gray says tomorrow," Joe said.

Once Sharon had swallowed down her bite of the s'more, she added, "She'll be so happy to see you."

"Hmm," Joey said.

"Aren't *you* happy?" their mother asked. "Happy to be here with us?"

Joey looked around, as though considering his answer. "Almost."

"Why almost?" their father asked.

"For the same reason as you," he said. "It's the most we can ever expect to be, don't you think? We'll—all of us—only ever be *almost* happy."

Daphne's hand moved to her lips.

Joe shook his head. "I disagree. I've made peace with the past. I know Kara is waiting for me in heaven, and right now, at this moment, I am completely happy."

Daphne couldn't prevent the tears from spilling down her cheeks and the frown from taking over her face.

"I won't tell you what my friend Judge William Clark says about heaven," Joey said.

"Even if there isn't a heaven," her father said. "I'm still at peace. We loved Kara and gave her a good life. We did the best we knew how to do."

"That's wonderful, Joe." Sharon patted her husband's hand.

"What about you?" Joe asked Sharon.

"I'm *almost* happy, too," she said, "but for a different reason than Joey. Once we're back home with our sweet Daphne and our sweet Joey, then I think I'll be *completely* happy, too."

Daphne covered her face with her hands and wept. Her stomach balled into a giant knot. Brock put an arm around her and caressed her back. She leaned into him.

Her sweet Mama! Daphne had poured all of her guilt over Kara's death into hating her. For two years, Daphne had been cold and rude and had tried everything she could to kill herself. Her mother hadn't deserved that. Daphne shuddered.

"We'll see," Joey said. "I'll believe it when I see it."

"He must be the doubting Thomas of the family," Dave said.

Daphne didn't reply but watched on as her family finished their s'mores. They talked about the stars—Joey knew every constellation, so he pointed to all the ones visible that night. A rush of childhood memories swept over Daphne, and she longed to be with her brother. She was glad he didn't mention his good friend Judge William Clark or the CIA again. And seeing him like his old self made her wish she had gone to Houston to visit him more often. She missed her big brother.

After some time, her father put a screen over the fire pit and hobbled after the others into the cabin.

"Now look at the monitor above that one," Stan said.

It showed the inside of the cabin, illuminated by their lantern. Her parents and Joey were arranging their bedding and taking turns using the restroom, which, thankfully, was not on a screen. Her mother helped her father climb onto his cot.

"The cabin doesn't have electricity," Stan explained. "And the only running water comes from a spigot outside. There's a toilet with a deep sewer, but that's it. It would cost us way too much to rebuild more than a crude cabin."

"Then how can it have a sprinkler system?" Daphne asked suspiciously.

"It's built into the slab," Dave explained. "The water shoots up from beneath. We *do* have running water down here."

"And obviously electricity," Vince added.

As she fluffed her pillow, her mother said, "Your doctor in Houston told me you destroyed all of your drawings and paintings. I meant to ask you about that earlier."

"Ask me what?"

"Why did you destroy them?" her mother clarified as she slipped off her shoes.

"Because creating them was a meaningless waste of time," he said, sitting down on his cot. "All art is."

"Art isn't a waste, son," her father said from his cot. "It brings a lot of joy to a lot of people."

"Like the books I read," Sharon added. "The stories help me deal with life."

"Art helps people escape their problems," Joe said.

"Not when it's stuck in an institution where no one ever sees it," Joey said.

"Then we need to do something about that." Sharon sat down on her cot and faced Joey. "We need to find you a gallery where you can exhibit your art."

"I don't know," Joey said. But then a few seconds later he asked, "Really?"

"Of course," Sharon said. "I have a cousin at Fort Davies with her own gallery. Maybe she would show your artwork there."

Joey sat up a little taller, and even in the dim light of the lantern, Daphne could see he looked happier.

Her mother put out the lantern and climbed beneath her blanket. Daphne could barely see her in the darkness.

After a few more minutes, they all said their goodnights, and the cabin grew quiet.

"How does the fire start?" Daphne asked.

"We control it from down here," Stan replied.

"We'll let them get settled first," Dave said.

"Just don't wait till they're sound asleep," Brock said. "Unless there's a smoke alarm in that cabin."

Neither Stan nor Dave answered. Daphne gnawed on the inside of her bottom lip, trying not to let the nausea overwhelm her. What if one of them got hurt? What if something went wrong? Dr. Gray and her staff couldn't control everything on this island, no matter how much they pretended otherwise. Just look what had happened on the helicopter.

Brock rubbed her back as she leaned against him watching the monitor.

"My parents do know about the fire, right?" Daphne asked.

"They were told that they were entering an exercise," Stan said. "I don't think they were given any details—just that Joey should save your dad."

Daphne sprang to her feet. "So they have no idea that their cabin is going to burn to the ground?"

"How fast can you access the cabin from down here?' Brock asked.

"This was a mistake," Dave said.

"Dr. Gray doesn't make mistakes," Stan said.

"Everyone makes mistakes," Daphne said. "You need to stop worshipping her like she's some kind of god. My dad and I almost died on that helicopter, and I'm not about to sit here and…I thought my parents knew about the fire. What if they fall asleep? Are you going to save them if Joey can't?"

"We're right below them," Stan said again. "Just sit down and watch. They're going to bed. It won't be long now."

Daphne crossed the room and tried to open the hatch door but found it locked. "You can't keep me in here. It's wrong. It's kidnapping. You're breaking the law. Let me out, Stan."

Brock joined her and tried to use brute force to open the hatch. "You know I can take you, man," Brock said. "At least let us be on standby, just in case."

"You *are* on standby," Dave said.

"Then show me the secret entrance," Brock demanded. "Show me or I'll…"

"Watch the screen," Stan said as he pushed a button on the control system on his desk. "The smoke is already visible, even in the dark."

Daphne bit down on her fingers, feeling utterly helpless.

Brock rushed at Stan and grabbed him by the shirt. "Tell me where the secret entrance is."

"I've already started the fire," Stan said. "If you hurt me, we won't be able to put it out. So back off."

Daphne returned to the desk and, with shaky hands, returned the headphones to her ears. "Will a smoke alarm go off in case they're already asleep?"

"No," Stan said. "No alarm."

"How can you do this?" Brock asked. "How can you lock us up and make us watch this?"

"Close your eyes," Dave said.

Brock turned and punched Dave in the face.

"Enough!" Stan said. "This part is critical."

"Are you okay?" Vince asked Dave.

"Yeah. It was nothing."

Daphne glanced back and saw Dave's cheek was flaming red and beginning to swell. But her eyes didn't stay on him long. The smoke thickened in the cabin, yet no one inside had moved.

"Why aren't they waking up?" Daphne asked.

"Give them time," Stan said.

"They don't have time!" Daphne objected.

Then, miracle of miracles, someone coughed.

"Joey?" came her mother's voice in the dark. "Joe! Joey! Wake up!"

"What?" Joey said.

Daphne could just make out his silhouette in the darkness. He stood up. An actual flame hopped like a red bird onto the curtain behind him.

"Let's get out of here," he said.

"Help me with your father," Sharon said.

The flames from the curtain ran up to the rafters and along one side of the wall. Then they caught onto her father's bedding.

"Oh my God!" Daphne cried. It was all happening so fast. *Too* fast!

Her mother and brother lifted her father from the cot and rushed to the door.

"It won't open," Sharon cried, pounding on the door in the frenzy of panic.

Daphne turned sharply toward Stan. "Why won't it open?"

"Just watch," he said.

"Open the door, Stan!" Daphne cried.

The flames had engulfed the inside of the cabin. All three of her family members were coughing and hacking.

"Come on, Joey," Stan murmured. "Think."

Joey grabbed one of their father's crutches and slammed it against the front window, breaking it. Then he and his mother helped her father out.

The monitor below saw them stumbling across the broken glass on the patio and into the side of the hill, away from the now blazing fire. The camera showed their three faces watching with looks of terror and awe as the flames shot up into the night sky, illuminating the mountainside.

Daphne sighed with relief and was overcome with tears. She just wanted this to all be over. She dropped her head down on the desk, racked with sobs. Just let it be over.

Brock patted and caressed her back, kissed the side of her head. "It's okay. Everything's okay. They're all safe."

"Now comes the part I haven't told you about," Stan said.

Daphne's head jerked up. "What?"

"Once they get in the jeep and head back to the resort, we're going to follow them," Dave explained.

"And?" Brock sneered.

"We're going to capture them," Stan said.

"What for?" Daphne asked.

"The Limuw ceremony," Stan replied.

Daphne stood up. "There's no way Joey can take that. He's too sick."

"Not Joey," Dave said.

"What?" Daphne glanced at all of their faces.

Stan stood up and removed his headphones. "Your mom. Let's go."

CHAPTER NINETEEN

Preparations

Was it bad that Daphne actually liked the idea of her mother playing Limuw? In spite of her reservations over Dr. Gray's dangerous and eccentric methods, Daphne still felt anger over the words her mother had said the morning they had found Kara, and she wanted to punish her mother.

"You mean you heard and did nothing?"

Her mother had also known to bring a scarf. Daphne kept telling herself that maybe her mother didn't know why she should bring it, but the resentment was there regardless.

Yet she and her mother had been through so much together on the island, and the healing process had begun. Her mother had proved that she loved Daphne and would do anything for her children. Wasn't that enough?

She followed Stan up the steel ladder from the tunnel in the side of Sierra Blanca and was glad when she was finally standing out in the open beneath the dark sky. The moon and stars shone brightly, and the air was fresh and cool, except for the ribbons of smoke from the burning cabin as they curled to the west of them. Although the wind chilled her, she was glad it carried the smoke away from them. Brock took her good hand, and they followed Stan down the trail and around the base of Sierra Blanca to a jeep hidden in the tall grass.

She squeezed in the backseat between Brock and Vince as Stan drove them around Central Valley and up the canyon ridge at a fast pace.

Daphne already knew the plan, but she was nevertheless anxious and scared.

They met up with the other jeep at the three-pronged fork in the road. Stan blew his horn and hollered out. Sharon pulled over near a bush of purple mountain glory and waited for Daphne to catch up to them.

"I'm awake!" Daphne shouted. "I've been looking for you!"

"Oh, sweetheart!" her mother cried.

"There was a fire," her father said from the passenger seat.

"I saw. I was worried sick. Hi, Joey!"

"Hi Daphne," Joey said. "My good friend Judge William Clark told me he likes your hair best long, but I think it looks good."

"Thanks." She gave him a hug.

Although he didn't hug her back, she was glad he didn't turn away from her like he often did. He let her hug him, and it felt great.

"Everybody okay?" Brock asked, approaching the jeep.

"Joey saved the day," Sharon said. "We were trapped in the burning cabin, and he thought of breaking us out through the window."

"You're probably still in shock," Brock said. "Why don't you guys climb in with Stan, and I'll drive Joey and Daphne."

"I'm okay to drive," Sharon said.

"No, Mama," Daphne insisted. "Please. I'm scared for you."

She and Brock helped her father from the jeep. Her mother grabbed the crutches from the back and transferred them to the other jeep. Vince jumped out to make more room for Daphne's parents in the backseat. Then he climbed into the passenger's side beside Brock. Daphne introduced him to Joey.

"We've met," Joey said.

Daphne had forgotten that a lot had happened in the two weeks she'd been out. As Brock drove the rest of the way to the resort, Daphne couldn't stop staring at her brother sitting beside her.

"It's so good to see you," she said.

"It's good to see you," he echoed.

"I'm sorry about the fire."

"Yeah."

"Were you scared?"

"Yeah."

She took his hand, and he didn't resist. "Listen, there's something I have to tell you."

He waited for her to continue.

"I went through therapy on this island," she said.

"You?"

She nodded. "And, at the end, the doctor shaved my head. That's why my hair is so short."

"Oh."

"At first I was mad about losing my hair. I liked my hair."

"So did I. So did my good friend Judge William Clark."

"But, in a strange way, it helped me overcome some of my problems." Had it? She couldn't decide whether or not she was lying to her brother. On the one hand, she was telling him this because she wanted him to accept what was about to happen to their mother; on the other hand, the Limuw ritual *had* helped her. It really *had*.

"That's good. Is the doctor going to shave my head, too?"

"Do you want her to?"

He shrugged.

"Well, she's going to shave Mom's."

"Oh."

"But Mom doesn't know yet, and she probably won't like it."

He seemed to consider this.

Daphne continued. "And then we will splash buckets of water on Mom, to punish her for hurting us."

"Has she hurt you?"

"She's hurt my feelings," Daphne said. "Has she ever hurt your feelings?"

The jeep reached the clearing and Brock parked, but Daphne didn't move to climb out. She waited for her brother's answer.

He nodded.

"When?"

"After grandpa died."

"What did she say?"

"She said I killed him, which was true. The CIA...no, not the CIA...I'm confused."

"It was an accident, Joey. Mom didn't mean that. She was in shock. She wasn't thinking properly."

"That's what the doctors say about me, but what I want to know is, what is *thinking properly*? What's the actual definition? That's a tricky question, isn't it?"

Daphne smiled and nodded. Then she climbed from the jeep and came around to Joey's side. "Come on. You're coming with me to get cleaned up. Then we're going to go back to sleep. Okay?"

He walked beside her. Brock and Vince followed behind.

"What about Mom and Dad?" Joey asked.

"They're getting ready for Mom's head-shaving. It's called the Limuw ritual. It's based on an island legend. You might find it interesting."

As they continued to her unit—all except Vince, who went to Joey's room to get him a change of clothes—she told Joey the story of Limuw.

"Hmm. That sounds metaphorical," Joey said. "My good friend Judge William Clark doesn't believe in literal resurrection."

While Joey showered, Brock stayed with Daphne, reassuring her.

"Am I doing the right thing?" she asked him as she made three sandwiches in the kitchenette. "Putting my mother through this?"

"Did it help you?" He poured them each a glass of water.

"Yes. I'm sure it did."

"Then you're doing the right thing."

"It's going to be hard to watch. But I want to watch. Ugh! Such mixed feelings. It's so confusing!"

"It felt good to throw the bucket of water on me. Admit it."

She smiled up at him. "Yeah. It did." Then she asked. "What about you? Did it feel good when you got to splash me?"

It was his turn to smile. "Yes."

She frowned.

"What?" he asked, circling his arms around her waist. "You really hurt me when you started blocking me out."

"I know. And I'm sorry. I just don't know how I feel about Dr. Gray and her methods. I feel like a hypocrite right now, going along, just like the Calibans."

"What Calibans?" Joey asked from the bedroom.

Brock stepped away and grabbed a glass of water. "Want something to drink?"

Joey took the offered glass. "What Calibans?"

"Oh, never mind," Daphne said. "Are you hungry?"

"I hate it when people do that to me," Joey said. "People are always doing that to me, as if I'm too stupid to understand. Well, I read *The Tempest*, and I'm well aware of who Caliban is. Now tell me what Calibans you are talking about."

It was funny how she could forget about the cameras and then suddenly remember she was being watched.

"Let's go sit down and I'll explain," Daphne said. "Want a sandwich?"

"No, thanks."

She and Brock took their sandwiches and sat on the striped chairs. Joey sat across from them on the edge of the bed.

"It's what I call Dr. Gray's helpers," Daphne explained.

"So you think they're her slaves?" Joey asked.

"Yes."

"Are they evil?"

"No," Daphne said. "And I'm not sure that Caliban would have been, either, if Prospero had treated him better."

"Prospero taught him language," Joey said. "Caliban was the one who tried to rape Miranda."

"I don't think he knew better," Daphne said. "He was like a wild animal, orphaned and alone, trying to make due. Prospero should have been more understanding."

Daphne ate her sandwich.

"Why don't you get some rest?" Brock said to Joey. "You take the bed. Daphne and I will sleep on the floor."

"Shouldn't I sleep in my own room?"

"We want to stay together," Daphne said.

Joey climbed to his feet. "But we'll see each other in the morning."

"I know, but I just got to see you." Daphne stood to embrace him again, and he tolerated it. "I'm not ready for you to leave me again."

"Will you be comfortable on the floor? I could sleep on the floor."

"We'll be fine," Daphne insisted.

"This rug is pretty plush," Brock said. "Can we have the comforter from the bed?"

Daphne finished her sandwich while the two boys arranged the bedding. Brock moved the coffee table to the side and spread the comforter across the rug. He left half of the comforter to cover up with. Joey had a sheet and throw on the bed.

Brock wedged one of the striped chairs against the doorknob.

"Why are you doing that?" Joey asked in a sleepy voice.

"It's just a precaution," Brock said. "We don't trust everyone around here."

Joey laughed.

"What's so funny?" Daphne asked.

"*I'm* the one who's supposed to be paranoid."

They all three laughed.

Daphne left on the light in the bathroom and then cracked the bathroom door so they wouldn't be enveloped in complete darkness. She wanted to see anything that might come their way, doubting she would sleep as she worried about her parents. She hoped and prayed that Stan had told her the truth about his plans for them.

CHAPTER TWENTY

Limuw

After breakfast, Daphne, Brock, and Joey headed to the amphitheater with the rest of the crowd. Unlike the others, however, they followed Cam backstage, where they changed into white hooded cloaks and waited for the ceremony to begin.

"Have you seen my parents yet?" she asked Cam. "Are they here?"

"Not yet." He winked. "Any minute now."

Daphne wished she hadn't eaten. Her stomach was in knots. She sat on a bench between Joey and Brock, unable to think and hoping to God her mother would forgive her.

After a few more minutes had passed, someone else in a cloak and hood hobbled onto the backstage with Cam's help. It was her father. Daphne jumped to her feet.

"Are you okay?" she asked him.

He nodded. "You?"

"Yes!" She hugged his neck. "How's mom?"

"She's still under the morphine. They're getting ready to start the ceremony."

She grabbed his hands. "Are we doing the right thing?"

"Did it help you?"

She nodded.

"Then you have your answer."

She hoped he was right.

When the music started, they took their seats on the long bench backstage and waited. They could hear Larry's voice ring out:

I cannot stand to see

How I've hurt those close to me;

Ribbons of despair run from their eyes, their eyes.

And ribbons of despair run from my eyes, my eyes.

Don't look at me

Those of you once close to me;

The fire inside you slowly dies, and dies.

And the fire inside me slowly dies, and dies.

When the song ended, Larry said, "Bring Limuw forward."

Daphne then saw her mother being carried in on a stretcher across the back of the stage to the altar. She appeared to be sleeping. Daphne's heart raged.

More music played, and another voice sang out in the Chumash language. Then Larry told the story of Limuw.

"Hutash has given us a ritual to bring Limuw back," he said at the end of it.

Now the cloaked figures on stage took scissors to her mother's hair. Tears fell down Daphne's cheek as she recalled her own horror when she awakened to find her hair gone. Cam had said, "It's just hair. It'll grow back." And he had been right. But the horror of losing it was still real.

An electric razor was taken to her mother's scalp, arms, and legs as Larry sang another song. Pete came backstage and brought Daphne a bucket filled with water. He handed buckets to Joey, Brock, and her father, too.

"It's almost time," Pete whispered. "Are you all ready? Don't chicken out on me, okay? Throw it like you mean it."

They all nodded. Daphne wanted to puke as she watched the cloaked performers on stage lay the oil-soaked cloth across her mother's body. The scent of the oil seemed to bring her mother to.

"What?" Sharon sat up and stared with horror at the crowd.

Daphne could see the side of her mother's horror-stricken face.

Brock squeezed Daphne's good hand. "It's going to be okay."

Her father patted her knee. "Here we go."

Her mother was carried by stretcher and forced onto a bench of rock, where the performers—Vince, Dave, Cam, and Bridget, cuffed her arms on either side of her to the rock wall. Only a white sheet covered her trembling body. Daphne was shocked by the sight of her mother's bald head and red-rimmed eyes. She looked like an old newborn baby.

Unlike Daphne, who had protested every step of the way during her Limuw ceremony, Sharon took everything in silent shock. She couldn't see Daphne and the others on the bench adjacent to her, but she was bound to know what was coming after having been on the other side of the fence. This reminder—that her mother had done it to her—gave Daphne the courage she needed to cover her face with the hood and follow Pete's instructions.

Daphne was the first to approach her mother's trembling, half-naked body. She lifted her hood and said through tears. "Mother, you shouldn't have blamed me for Kara's death." Then she took her bucket of water and splashed it on her mother's face.

Her mother nodded and sputtered through the water and her own tears, "You're right, sweet girl. You're absolutely right!"

That made Daphne feel like a worm. She walked away to avoid crumbling at her mother's feet.

Joey approached their mother next. Daphne watched from a distance. "You shouldn't have blamed me for Grandpa's death."

Joey had a hard time splashing their mother. He emptied the bucket on the floor by her feet. Pete gave him another full bucket and instructed him to "let her have it."

Joey did his best. Then he joined Daphne on the side of the action and watched as Brock and their father had their turns. Brock stood before Sharon's frail, limp body and threw the water at her, holding nothing back.

"You hurt Daphne," he said. "And you hurt me because of it."

Sharon closed her eyes and nodded, trembling and soaked.

Then it was Joe's turn.

"I didn't always listen to you," he said gently. "But you didn't always tell me things, either." His lips started quivering as he said, "You have to talk to me, Sharon. You have to include me in things. You have to tell me when you notice something's wrong. I might have done something. I might have saved our girl."

Sharon turned paler than snow. "You blame me for Kara's death?"

"I blame both of us," he said as he poured the water on her lap and turned away.

After they had finished, and while others took turns splashing Sharon, they were led to separate benches to await their turns to be splashed.

Larry's voice rang out. "You've been purified, purged of all wrongdoing, and are clean, pure as a newborn infant."

Daphne's arms were shackled to the wall on either side of her, her broken arm stretched awkwardly. She felt helpless and frightened, even though she knew what would happen. But her doubts about Dr. Gray and her staff made her question whether some new surprise might await her. Maybe she would learn that all of this had been one more exercise designed for *her,* and everyone—including Brock and her family—had been in on it.

As her mother was led to stand before Daphne, Larry added, "Now it's your turn, Limuw. It's your turn to inflict the punishment and to purify others."

Daphne's mother shook all over. "I can't do it."

Larry picked up the bucket and thrust it toward Sharon. "Come on. Hit her with it."

Sharon shook her head, backing away.

Tears streamed down Daphne's face. "Please, Mama! Do it! I should have forgiven you!"

"I am the parent. I should have known better."

"You were in shock! We all say things we don't mean!" Daphne's teeth chattered and snot dripped from her nose. She wanted to wipe her face, but she couldn't. "I know you didn't mean it! I'm so sorry I didn't forgive you!"

Sharon stood quivering like a leaf, unable to take the bucket. "No."

"It was easier to be mad at you than to accept what happened!" Daphne cried. "I poured all my loss, all my pain, into *hating* you. I'm so sorry, Mama. I'm so sorry. I love you so much. I beg of you to hit me with the water. Please!"

With shaking hands, Sharon took the bucket and gently poured it over Daphne's head. Daphne cried into the water as it cascaded down her face, and, in so doing, she felt all the guilt, the hate, the pain, and the loss washing away. She smiled up at her mother, and her mother smiled down at her. Then something amazing happened. They both began to laugh.

After the ceremony, they were all brought on stage where the members of the audience could, if they wanted, kiss the hands of Daphne, Brock, and her family. This had not been a part of Daphne's ceremony, so she hadn't expected it.

"You are loved," some of them said.

Even though she was soaked and shivering, Daphne was warmed by this overwhelming show of affection.

"You are loved."

Most of the regulars did it and a dozen of the older crowd, including Mary Ellen, Philip, Kelly, and Larry.

"You are loved."

By the time the audience had dispersed and they were left alone with Hortense Gray and a handful of regulars, Daphne felt like rubber. Physically and emotionally drained, all she wanted to do was sleep.

Her family members and Brock were each given a silver chain bracelet, and Daphne was given one, as well, to replace the one she had thrown away.

"It signifies the pain that binds us, that holds us back," Dr. Gray said. "But it also signifies the bonds of fellowship that hold us all together."

They were instructed to return to their rooms and rest. Later that evening, they would discuss their travel plans for getting off the island.

Daphne embraced her mother. They held one another for a long time and shed more tears. They also laughed. At one time, they were laughing and crying at the same time. Daphne also hugged her father and Joey. Then she took Brock's hand, and they all made their way from the amphitheater to their units.

Anxious to get out of her wet cloak, Daphne climbed into the hot shower. As the water massaged her neck and back—she had to keep her cast dry, but that didn't mean the rest of her had to suffer—she wondered again how she felt about Dr. Gray and her methods. Wasn't she glad she had come to the island? In spite of everything, wasn't she grateful?

She had just slipped on a clean t-shirt and comfy shorts when she heard a knock at the door. Expecting Brock, she opened the door and was surprised to find Giovanni.

"Oh my gosh!" She gave him a hug. "Come in."

He didn't look happy as he stepped inside, wringing his hands.

She closed the door behind him. "What's wrong?"

"You gotta take me with you," he said. "I want off this island."

"Come over here and sit down." She motioned to one of the striped chairs. After they had each taken one, she said, "Now tell me what's wrong."

"I can't believe you," he said. "Just two weeks ago, we were running for our lives. What's happened to you?"

"Nothing, I…"

"She's brainwashed you."

"I'm not brainwashed."

"You're even wearing one of their bracelets."

She twirled it nervously at her wrist. "I'm not brainwashed. I just understand everything better now."

He shook his head, anger flaring in his face. "There's nothing you can say that will make this place okay. They play with people here like they're nothing."

"They're trying to help people."

"They use us like puppets for their own purposes. Taking advantage of orphans."

"I'm not an orphan."

He searched her eyes. "You gotta help me. I have no one else."

Daphne put her good hand on his. "Listen. It may seem scary right now, but I promise you, it is so worth it. You will be grateful in the end."

A bad taste filled Daphne's mouth, because she realized at that moment that she *did* sound exactly like the Calibans.

CHAPTER TWENTY-ONE

The Judgment of Hortense Gray

After Giovanni left, Daphne had just gotten comfortable in one of the striped chairs with the TV on, hoping for some mindless down time, when another knock came at the door. Was it Giovanni with one more thing to add? Brock? She looked through the window to find Cam waving back at her.

"Cam, hey." She opened the door and let him in. "What's up?"

"We actually have one more surprise for you tonight," he said with a gleam in his eyes.

"Oh, no, no, no." She backed away from him. "No more surprises."

"You'll love this one."

"I doubt that."

"This is the event everyone here looks forward to the most—even more than the Limuw ceremony."

"I'm not going anywhere with you." There was no way she would allow herself to get pulled into another game. She was almost off the island. And yet…And yet the thought of leaving behind the thrill of the games did leave her feeling somewhat deflated.

"Please. Come on. I promise…"

"No. Now, stop." She collapsed into one of the striped chairs.

"Pretty please?"

She turned to look at him. Part of her was curious. What more could they possibly have in store for her?

No. She would not go. She needed to return to normalcy.

When she didn't answer, he groaned. "I guess Stan was right."

Before she could reply, a group of people flooded the room. They wore black ski masks and black sweats. She recognized them beneath their garb and inwardly laughed, thinking how hot they must be. Until the sun went down, the temperature hovered in the mid-eighties on the island. They had to be sweating as the regulars grabbed her by the arms.

"Come on," she scoffed. "I've had enough. Vince? I know that's you. Hello, Stan. Hi, Dave. Bridget? Those sweats don't do you justice, girlfriend." She noticed Greg and Emma weren't among them.

She was about to taunt them more when she was gagged with a red bandana and a bag was slipped over her head. She struggled against them as they bound her wrists behind her back, in spite of her cast, and moved her forward. This was ridiculous. She kicked at them, but they dodged her and dragged her from the room.

Then the horrible thought that they would do something like this to Joey, her parents, or Brock immobilized her. She closed her eyes and sought out Cam's smell, trying to find him among the others, willing him to help her, but he did nothing to stop this ridiculous abduction.

She was made to walk up the sidewalk. She could tell by the incline that they were headed away from the beach and toward the clearing where the jeeps were parked. She wondered if there were others out and about watching them. If so, would someone intervene? She made as much noise as she could, just in case.

Now they ascended the steps toward the amphitheater. So their little event would take place there, huh? Another Limuw ceremony? *Please don't let it be Joey's*. Daphne cringed.

She was led down what she knew were the steps along the amphitheater seats. Why cover her head when she could tell where they were going? She tried to protest, but the gag made all her efforts sound insane.

When she heard someone giggle, she became infuriated. The games were fun and exciting, but always at the cost of another, and right now, she was paying the price.

If she had had doubts about leaving the island before, they were totally gone now. She wanted the hell off.

Down the last step, and then up a few more, the group led her into what she could sense, even beneath the bag, was darkness. They were backstage, where the buckets were used in the Limuw ceremony. Daphne was forced down on her knees on the hard, damp, rock floor. She smelled something like incense, heard whispering.

She did not like being blinded from what was happening around her as she listened to the shuffle of feet and more whispers. After a few more minutes of this miserable anticipation, the bag was lifted from her head. Even with the gag between her teeth, Daphne gasped.

Seated on the rock benches before her, with their hands shackled above them just as Daphne had once been, were Mary Ellen, Hortense Gray, and Lee Reynolds. They were wearing the same white tunics used in the Limuw ceremony. At first, Daphne thought that maybe the Calibans were rebelling against the Purgatorium, but the faces of the three prisoners were without expression. They had been here before.

Larry stepped forward and said to Daphne, "You have been treated as a patient by a team of psychologists—Dr. Mary Ellen Rose, Dr. Hortense Gray, and Dr. Lee Reynolds. They have used experimental methods to help you overcome your clinical depression, posttraumatic stress syndrome, and suicidal tendencies. They have treated your family as well, in an effort to help all of you overcome the past and begin the healing process. In doing so, they may have crossed some ethical lines. It is your turn to judge them, to determine whether their methods have been helpful or hurtful. If you find their methods have been more hurtful than helpful, you're to throw on each of them a bucket of water. If, however, you feel the opposite is true, you're to lay one of these roses at their feet. It's your choice, Daphne.

"But before you make your decision, consider both the means and the ends. Without a doubt, you and your family are better off psychologically than before undergoing the therapy. You must ask yourself if these successful ends justify the means in which they were achieved.

"One more thing. We recorded a debriefing interview with each of your family members and with Brock. We will play back a segment of each of these as you make your decision. The first is from Brock."

Over the same speaker system previously used for the music came the voice of Hortense Gray: "Brock, have you noticed any changes in Daphne since her arrival here?"

Brock's voice, surprisingly low and gentle, came next: "She's a stronger person. I was shocked when I saw her diving off the cliffs into the crashing waves. She's always been athletic and a great swimmer, but she's never been very determined or driven. Seeing her fight to save me and her family was incredible. Even with a broken arm, she knocked it out of the ballpark."

Daphne bit down on the gag, holding back tears. She supposed what Brock had said was true. After Kara's death, Daphne hadn't cared too much about anything, and it had been an amazing feeling on the island to care about something, to care about getting herself and her loved ones to safety. And, when she thought about it, she supposed she was pretty darn proud of what she had been able to do.

Larry interrupted her thoughts. "Now we'll hear from your brother."

Dr. Gray asked a different question. "And what about Daphne? Do you think she let you down?"

Joey's voice came over the sound system, strong and clear and amazingly confident. "When she stopped coming to see me in Houston, I got depressed. It felt like she didn't care about me anymore. I looked forward to seeing my parents, but I was always disappointed when she wasn't with them."

Daphne's heart seemed to stop.

"But seeing her here on the island," Joey paused.

"Go on," Hortense said.

Daphne looked at the doctor shackled across from her, and Hortense Gray stared back.

Joey said with a laugh, "She couldn't stop hugging me."

"And how did that make you feel?" Hortense asked.

"Great," Joey said. "It made me feel great, like she's forgiven me."

"Do you think she blamed you for what happened to Kara?"

"Of course," Joey said. "Why wouldn't she?"

Tears streamed down Daphne's cheeks. *But I don't blame you, Joey. I don't!*

"You know the answer to that," Dr. Gray said. "Your illness. Many victims of schizophrenia have acted in ways outside of their control. It's easier to believe you could have done something to prevent Kara's death than to accept that you, too, were a victim."

"Do you think Daphne sees it that way?" Joey asked.

"I know she does," Hortense replied.

Daphne's body shook with sobs. Poor Joey. Her sweet brother thought she blamed him all this time.

Larry spoke up again, bringing Daphne from her thoughts. "The next excerpt comes from your father."

Dr. Gray's voice came again over the loudspeaker: "Do you think she's changed, then?"

"Yes," her father replied.

"In a good way?" Hortense asked.

"Absolutely," Joe said. "She's more resolved and less resigned. I think that's it in a nutshell. She'd become empty, and now she's got a fire in her belly. I see the flames in her eyes."

"Like she's been resurrected," Hortense said.

"Exactly." Her father's voice cracked. Daphne could tell he was fighting tears. "Thank you for giving me my little girl back."

Daphne's throat went dry. She wished she could go back in time and erase her behavior after Kara's death. She wished she could have been stronger, like she felt now. Yes, she *was* stronger *and* more resolved. She really felt she could take anything and fight back.

Larry lifted his finger and said, "The last excerpt comes from your mother's debriefing. After this, you will be asked to judge."

As soon as the recording came on, Daphne could hear her mother sobbing.

"I've got to stop wishing that," her mother said.

"Yes," Hortense said. "Once words are spoken, you can't take them back. But you can forgive yourself, just as Daphne has forgiven you."

"I know that now," her mother said. "And I thank you, doctor. I can finally see it in Daphne's eyes. I didn't think…" her mother broke into more sobbing before she regained her composure and said, "I really didn't think she would ever forgive me, or ever love me again. She pushed me away. She would rather die than be near me…"

Daphne collapsed onto her bottom. *Mama!* If it weren't for the gag, she would cry out.

"But now you know differently, yes?" Dr. Gray asked.

"Yes. I can see it in her eyes. I really can. She *does* love me, and she *does* forgive me, and I really think, because of you, we have a chance to move on."

Daphne closed her eyes and was racked with sobs. Someone removed her gag and unbound her wrists, and she covered her face and wept. Her poor mama. Her poor, sweet mama. Daphne was glad her mother finally knew that Daphne did love and forgive her.

Larry brought her from her thoughts. "Now it's time for you to make your decision, Daphne. Do these doctors get the bucket or the rose?"

Daphne looked around and noticed a crowd surrounded her. In addition to the regulars—both the young and older crowds—were her parents, Joey, and Brock. They were crying, too. Even Joey shed tears. He smiled back at her and gave her a wave. She waved back.

She looked at the three buckets of water in front of her and the one pot with the three roses. Without hesitation, she climbed to her feet and, with trembling hands, took up the flowers and laid them at the feet of the three doctors.

CHAPTER TWENTY-TWO

Goodbye

Daphne felt uneasy as she, her family, and Brock ate dinner at the table with Hortense Gray and Arturo Gomez. She could feel the regulars watching them, and, at another table, Giovanni sat with Bridget eyeing Daphne with his looks of desperation.

Although Cam and most of her new friends were among the regulars at the table nearby, Gregory and Emma were absent. She wondered if they were off spending time together or if they were part of another exercise for someone else. In any case, she hoped for the opportunity to say goodbye to them. They hadn't been at her mother's Limuw ceremony, and she hadn't spoken to Greg since the night he had told her to get her family off the island.

"So be ready right after breakfast," Dr. Gray said. "Roger and Stan will come by and give you all a lift to Prisoners Harbor."

"The boat comes at ten a.m. sharp," Arturo added. "You don't want to be late."

Daphne's parents nodded.

"Of course not," Joe said.

"I'll come to San Antonio once every two months to check on Joey's status," Dr. Gray said. "Here's my card with my contact information, in case you need to reach me in between visits."

Sharon, who, unlike Daphne, wore her bald head exposed like a badge of courage, took the card from the doctor's outstretched hand. "Thank you."

Joe asked, "Do you have an office in San Antonio, then?"

"I make house calls," the doctor replied.

Daphne's eyes widened with surprise, not sure how she felt about Hortense Gray coming to her home, but she said nothing.

"That's convenient," Joey said, beaming.

"My fee is on the back of my card."

Sharon turned it over and grimaced. "Yikes." She handed it to her husband.

Arturo said, "You get what you pay for."

"Still less expensive than that place in Houston," Joe said.

Joey had been *living* there, so Daphne would *hope* the house call was less expensive.

"We're just glad to have our Joey at home again," Sharon said.

"And you're always welcome to come back to the resort," Arturo Gomez added. "Anytime. You don't even have to make a reservation."

"Especially if Daphne decides to volunteer," Dr. Gray added. "And Brock, too, of course."

"Thank you," Brock said.

He and Daphne exchanged looks. She wouldn't mind returning and keeping an eye on Cam, Giovanni, and Emma, but she also wanted to spend some time with Joey. More importantly, she had decided she wanted to get her G.E.D. and maybe even enroll in college. Trinity University had offered her a swimming scholarship before she dropped out, just like the one Brock received. She wondered if there was any way that could be put back on the table.

As Daphne bussed her tray and prepared to head back to her unit with her family and Brock, Cam came up behind her.

"Hey," he said.

"Hey." She smiled back at him.

"Me and some of the others want to give you a going away party on the beach tonight. It's just the younger crowd—no offense, Mr. and Mrs. Janus."

"None taken," Daphne's father said.

"That sounds like a nice idea," Sharon added. "You two should go." She meant Daphne and Brock.

"Joey, man, you should come, too," Cam said.

"Okay," Joey said.

"Sure," Daphne added. "What time?"

"Sundown. About nine-thirty or so."

"See ya there," Brock said.

"See ya there," Joey echoed.

A bonfire cast light and shadows on the beach below. From the boardwalk, Daphne could see most the regulars already down there, sitting in folding chairs on the sand, drinking, talking, laughing, and roasting marshmallows over one of the numerous flames bursting from a huge pile of scrap wood.

"What exactly are we going to do down there?" Joey asked, sounding as though he had reservations about joining the party.

"Just talk," Daphne said.

"About what?" Joey asked.

"Anything. Nothing in particular."

"It's a party," Brock said, leading the way down the steps. "Just relax and enjoy yourself. Have a Coke and make a s'more."

"Okay," Joey said. "It's just that me and my good friend Judge William Clark never particularly enjoyed parties. I'm just not used to them."

"Maybe you'll enjoy this one," Daphne said.

"Maybe."

As they neared the group, the sound of music poured from someone's radio, and Dave sang along to it in a loud tenor voice.

"Daph!" Cam called from the other side of Dave and Vince. He circled around the singer and greeted Daphne with a hug. "Hey, Joey." Cam hugged Joey next. "Brock." He shook Brock's hand.

"What, I don't get a hug?" Brock teased.

Cam blushed and hugged him. "No offense, man. I grew up with these two. They're like family."

"No worries."

Bridget and Giovanni sat together on a log on the other side of the fire—a bit too closely, Daphne thought. She didn't like the idea of Hortense baiting Giovanni with a pretty girl, especially one who was supposedly dating Cam. And Cam should have seemed concerned, but he didn't. Instead, he led them over to a group of folding canvas chairs on the other side of Vince and Dave where Stan sat on top of an ice chest.

"Want something to drink?" Stan asked them.

"I'm fine," Daphne said.

Brock took a Sprite.

Sitting on the sand on the other side of the ice chest were two girls Daphne hadn't yet met, but Brock and Joey seemed to know them. They must have met while Daphne was asleep in the infirmary. Stan introduced them as Jeannette and Paula—new arrivals.

"Where are Emma and Gregory?" Daphne asked Stan.

Stan shrugged. "Probably making out somewhere."

Daphne turned to Cam. "I haven't seen either of them since before I tried to leave the island."

Vince flashed a roasted marshmallow on a skewer in Cam's face. "Want it?"

"Yeah, sure, man. Thanks." Cam grabbed graham crackers and chocolate from a basket on the ground and eased the marshmallow from the skewer. He took a bite. "Mmm. You guys gotta try one."

"I'll take one," Joey said.

Cam pushed a new marshmallow onto the end of the skewer and handed it over to him. "There you go, buddy."

Joey sat in one of the folding chairs and held the skewer over the bonfire.

Dave snagged Vince's towel and took off running toward the shoreline.

"Hey!" Vince jumped up. "Give that back!"

"Make me!" Dave shouted.

Vince chased Dave toward the water.

"Good," Cam said. "More chairs." He took the chair Vince had been sitting in. Then he picked up the radio and tried to find a different station.

Brock sat in a chair next to Joey, leaving an empty one between him and Cam for Daphne. Daphne didn't take it, though.

She leaned closer to Cam and whispered, "Tell me the truth about Greg and Emma."

"I honestly don't know," Cam whispered back. "I know he and his mom haven't been getting along. That's it."

A shrill scream came from the water. It sounded like Vince. Daphne thought maybe Dave had thrown him in the cold sea, but when the scream was followed by another, and then by Dave shouting, she knew something was wrong—either that, or a new game had begun, maybe for one of the new arrivals.

"Help!" Dave shouted. "Over here!"

Daphne and Cam took off running. Brock caught up to her just as they neared Vince and Dave hunched over something washed up on the beach.

It was Emma.

Daphne fell to her knees in the wet sand as the last bit of a shallow wave swept up to her before ebbing back into the dark sea. It took with it some of the blood covering Emma's limp, bruised body. The rest of the teens gathered around in shocked silence. As they examined her battered body, which had clearly been pummeled, no one wanted to ask the questions they must have all been thinking. Did she jump from the bluff? And if so, did she intend to kill herself?

"Someone get Dr. Gray," Stan finally said. "Vince. You're the fastest runner. You go."

Vince took off like a track star.

"Poor Kara," Daphne said. Then her breath caught. "I mean Emma. Poor Emma."

Her face blazed with heat as everyone looked at her. Brock wrapped a comforting arm around her shoulders.

"Come away," he said.

When she stood up, she noticed Joey was as white as a sheet.

"Are you okay?" she asked him.

"You called her Kara," he said.

"I know." Tears flowed from her eyes. "I know. I'm sorry. I was in shock. I wasn't thinking properly."

"There's no such thing," he said.

"No such thing as what?" she asked.

"As thinking properly," he replied. "There's just thinking and not thinking."

"Then I wasn't thinking," Daphne corrected. "I was reacting and not thinking."

Joey nodded and the three of them went back to their seats by the fire where Daphne fought to rein in the unending tears.

Soon the adults arrived—Hortense, Arturo, Lee, and Philip. They made the kids return to their rooms. Brock stayed over with Daphne, but even in his comforting arms, she could find no sleep.

The next day, they held a memorial service on the beach for Emma after breakfast. Daphne wondered what had happened to the remains. There was a rumor that Dr. Gray had burned them on the bonfire last night, and when Daphne asked Cam about it in low whispers during the service, he said Emma had no family. Emma's mother had turned custody over to Dr. Gray.

Daphne also wondered why Greg hadn't shown up for the service. Was he crying his eyes out alone in his room, or would his body be the next to wash up on the shore?

Most of the adults had said their goodbyes to Daphne and her family after the memorial service, but Dr. Gray and Roger had come along to Prisoners Harbor, as had most of the regulars and Giovanni.

Dr. Gray shook each of their hands and reminded Daphne's parents that she would see them in two months. Her parents thanked the doctor over and over, both of them with tears in their eyes. Daphne thanked her, too.

Dr. Gray stepped aside so Roger could follow suit, shaking their hands and telling them it was a pleasure to meet them. "Come back again and we'll look for some more birds," he said.

Then Daphne was surrounded by the regulars, each offering her a hug—all but Emma (of course) and Gregory. Cam asked her again to come back as a volunteer, and she promised to think about it.

When, last of all, Giovanni came up for a hug, he whispered in her ear, "Come back for me. Please don't leave me here."

Daphne frowned and said simply, "Goodbye, Giovanni."

Dragging their rolling bags behind them, Daphne, Brock, and her family walked across the wooden slats to the catamaran waiting to take them home. They waved again once they were settled and pulling away from the pier. As they rounded the eastern side of the island, Daphne was overwhelmed with mixed emotions. She hated that island, and she loved it, too.

They made one more stop—at Scorpion Anchorage—to pick up a few more passengers, mostly men with huge backpacks. Once they were loaded, the boat eased away from the pier and headed out to open sea toward the mainland.

Brock held her waist as they watched the dolphins swimming alongside the boat. Daphne's parents and brother all wore thoughtful expressions on their faces. They looked happy. Daphne smiled and believed that she, too, was happy. *Completely* happy.

After they had reached the port at Ventura and had exited the boat, one of the men with the huge backpacks from Scorpion Anchorage sidled up to Daphne.

"Are you Daphne?" he asked her.

She bent her brows in surprise. The man didn't look at all familiar to her.

"Who are you?" Brock asked.

"Coming, Daphne?" her mother called from the end of the pier.

"Someone asked me to give this to you," the man thrust a folded piece of paper into Daphne's good hand and walked away without looking back.

"What is it?" Brock asked her.

"Our shuttle is here," Joe called out to them.

Daphne and Brock rushed to the end of the pier and along the sidewalk to the shuttle. Once their bags had been taken and stored in back, Daphne sat in a seat beside Brock and opened the paper. Inside, scrawled in pencil, she read:

Daphne,

You've got to help me. Please come back with the FBI and help me and Emma get away from my deranged parents. They won't let us leave. I have a trust fund from my father. I will give you whatever you want.

Yours,

Greg

Daphne looked up at Brock. "Oh my God."

"You don't think it's another exercise," Brock said.

"I don't know what to think." Either Greg didn't know Emma had died, or he had written this note before it had happened. "I think we're going to have to go back to the island."

"You've got to be kidding me," he said.

But she wasn't kidding. And, surprisingly, the thought of returning filled her with relief. She had never felt more alive than she had felt at the Purgatorium. Her heart raced with the thrill of anticipation. She didn't want it to be over.

"Living art," she murmured, piecing something together. "That's what Dr. Gray meant about living art."

"What are you talking about?"

"When a book ends, the story is over, dead. Same thing when the curtain closes, when the lights come on in the movies, or when a song ends. Art in a painting is dead. It's frozen. But this island, this therapy gives you an experience that stays alive as long as you want it to. It's not real—it's art. Living art."

"Wait a minute," Brock said. "Are you for or against Dr. Gray?"

"I don't know yet. It depends on what I find out."

"Are we going to tell the FBI?" he asked her.

"Not yet," she said. "I don't want to get everyone in trouble if Greg's just pissed at his mom and if Emma's death was really a suicide."

"We?" he asked.

"You're coming with me aren't you?" she asked.

"I've got to go back to work," he said. "I can't afford to take off any more days. And I really don't like the idea of you going back without the FBI."

Daphne reread the letter over and over. Somehow, some way, she would get Brock to understand and convince her parents to let her return. She had to get back to the island and discover the rest of the story.

THE END

Thank you for reading my story. If you enjoyed it, please consider leaving a review. Reviews help other readers to find my books, which helps me.

Please enjoy this excerpt from the next book, *The Calibans*.

CHAPTER ONE

Scorpion Anchorage

Daphne had come all this way, had deceived just about everyone she knew to make it happen, and she couldn't even climb out of the dang boat onto the pier at Scorpion Anchorage.

Her backpack was too heavy. How did she expect to traipse around the entire island with it? Another wave of panic shimmied down her spine, and that voice that had been haunting her since she had made her decision to return repeated its mantra: *You don't know what you're doing.*

A flock of seagulls cried out overhead, as though they were laughing at her.

She frowned at the captain as he handed over her propane canister, which had been stored on the ride over.

Great. One more thing to add to her load.

"I'm gonna have to leave some things here, I guess—if that's okay." She squinted against the bright sun.

He didn't reply, but since he didn't say no, she eased the pack down on a bench, pulled her arms free, and began the frustrating process of deciding which lifesaving items she could live without.

She wasn't going to give up her sleeping bag. She'd rather starve. Her new Jetboil stove was another item she couldn't do without. Plus it was small—just a two-cup mug that attached to a small propane canister. The beef jerky, oatmeal packs, protein bars, and dried pasta mixes weren't heavy. Should she chuck some of the canned goods? Hmmm. Maybe she really didn't need all these beans and canned chicken.

No. She could imagine Kara shaking a finger: Scaling the bluffs and trudging along in the elements required protein.

The portable phone chargers had to stay. How else would she capture the evidence she needed to bring this place down?

What about her poetry journal? No. She couldn't live without it. It would stay in the pack.

She had bought a tent large enough for two people, because she couldn't stand the coffin-like feeling of a one-person tent. She could probably go without it, but it was the only place where she could ever be sure she wasn't on camera. Her hand circled around the hammer she planned to use to drive in the stakes. It was pretty darn heavy. Maybe she could use rocks instead.

She handed it over to the captain. "You can have this."

He took the hammer without comment as she rummaged around for something else to leave behind.

The captain eyed her jugs of water. "There's fresh water on the campgrounds."

She knew that, but what the captain didn't know was that she wasn't going to be staying on the campgrounds for long.

"The water is your heaviest weight," the captain said. "Dump those, and you'll manage better."

As she was considering the captain's advice, another boat approached the harbor. Daphne nearly shrieked when she saw Dr. Hortense Gray standing among the passengers, holding onto the railing and looking out to shore, like a spider on the edge of its web.

Daphne dropped to her knees and hid behind the side of the catamaran.

The chances of being recognized by Dr. Gray and her staff were pretty slim. Daphne had dyed her hair blonde and was wearing a baseball cap and sunglasses. Her brother Joey's baggy sweatshirt and jeans helped to hide her physique. Besides, no one would be looking for Daphne. No one was expecting her. She blended with the other campers and hikers just fine. But she didn't want to take any chances—especially before she'd even gotten off the boat.

The captain's brows slanted together.

"I don't want to be seen by that woman," Daphne explained. "Please don't give me away. Please?"

"I'm on a tight schedule, miss," the captain said.

All of the other passengers had already gone ashore.

"I'll give you fifty bucks," Daphne said.

His eyes lit up. "Fifty bucks?"

Daphne fished in her back pocket for her wallet, nearly dropping her phone. She pulled out two twenties and a ten and handed them over, considering it money well spent. No way was she going to let this mission be spoiled before it ever began. Too much time, money, and energy had already been put into it.

"Fine." The captain took the cash and returned to his cockpit.

Daphne listened for the other boat to pull away from the pier. Dr. Gray would be circling around to Prisoners Harbor and docking there, which is exactly why Daphne was getting off *here*.

Even Greg didn't know Daphne was returning to the island.

When he'd called her in January, she was at first shocked, then suspicious, and, finally, sympathetic. She had agreed to meet him at a small café one Saturday afternoon, as long as she could bring Brock. It had been a week before Christmas.

Greg was seated at a corner booth when she and Brock walked in. Greg looked thin, nervous, and tired. Dark bags hung beneath his eyes.

"Thanks for coming," he said.

"Glad to see you, man." Brock offered Greg a fist-bump.

"My God." Daphne slid into the booth across from him, unable to peel her eyes away from his gaunt face.

Brock sat next to her. "You don't look so good."

Greg gave them a half smile and shrugged. "No, I guess not."

"How did you get off the island?" Daphne asked.

He had refused to tell her anything over the phone.

"When I found out about Emma…" he stopped for a minute to collect himself.

Daphne bit her lip, feeling awkward. "I never got to tell you how sorry I was for your loss."

"Me, too, man," Brock added.

"So you know." Greg wiped his eyes, which had filled with tears. "Well, I had no reason to stay. I left, right after you did, I guess. Had to beg for transportation, but I got away."

A waitress asked if she could get them something to drink. They all ordered water.

"What about your mom?" Daphne asked, when the waitress had left.

"Like I said on the phone, I don't want her to know where I am."

"Have you talked to her since you left?" Brock asked.

"No. And you have to promise not to say anything to her."

Daphne was worried about how agitated he'd become. "We promise. We won't say a word."

"You don't have to worry about me," Brock assured him. "I never see her."

"But *you* do," Greg said to Daphne. "She comes to treat your brother. Does she ever talk about me?"

Daphne shook her head. Dr. Gray had come to see Joey twice: once in September and again in November. She was due to return in two weeks. "Whenever I ask how you are, she says you're fine."

Greg laughed, but it wasn't pleasant. The sound from his throat was more a like a cackle. It sounded both evil and heartbreaking.

"I'm sorry," she added, feeling guilty for having allowed herself to forget about the traumas of the Purgatorium. Her brother, Joey, seemed almost like his old self—like before he had accidentally killed their grandfather. Daphne had gone back to school. Her parents were happier. She and Brock were getting along great.

It had been easy to forget.

The waitress returned with their water and asked if they wanted anything to eat. Daphne and Brock ordered the special—chicken-fried steak.

"I don't have any money." Greg looked down at his hands.

"It's on us," Brock said. "Get whatever you want."

Greg thanked them and ordered the special, too.

Daphne peeked over the rail of the catamaran to confirm that the other boat had left. She sighed with relief. It was gone.

"I'm going to be late to my next stop," the captain complained from his cockpit.

Deciding to take his advice, she left the water jugs on the floor of the boat. She had two liters in the bladder of her backpack and lots of iodine tablets for when she got to the stream in Central Valley. She slipped her arms through the straps, hefted the beast onto her back, and climbed onto the pier.

It was time to begin.

With the sun beating down on her from high noon, the shade trees and flat dirt path were a relief as she walked the half- mile trek to her campsite. The park office in Ventura had assigned her to number thirteen. It had been an easy number to remember, because it had been Kara's age when she died.

On the way to her site, Daphne passed two families with younger children, a couple in their twenties, and two groups of men. It was the first Saturday of spring break, so she had expected there would be people, and that was good, because it helped her to blend in.

Her new boots felt comfortable, but the waterproof socks made her hot, and she wanted out of her sweatshirt now that she was off the boat. The wind wasn't nearly as bad here as she remembered it being on the other side of the island. She dropped her pack on a picnic table at a vacant site and stripped off the shirt, having remembered to dress in layers. In fact, she wore a one-piece bathing suit beneath her clothes so she could easily bathe in the stream without stripping down. Then she lathered some sunscreen on her arms. She'd learned her lesson from the last trip.

As she continued on her way, she sipped the water from the tubing that led to the plastic bladder in her pack and thought more about her conversation with Greg at the café back in San Antonio.

"I came here for three reasons," Greg said, once the waitress had left to fill their order. "First, to tell you about Emma. I wasn't sure if you knew."

"We were there when they found her," Daphne said, recalling that night on the beach. The memory of Emma's black and blue body lying on the shore in a heap made her shiver. "I'm so sorry. Do you know what happened?"

Greg sucked in his lips, fighting tears. "We were going to make a run for it during your mom's Limuw ceremony." He took a napkin and patted the beads of sweat forming on his face. "Emma was still recovering from her gunshot wounds. I should have known she wasn't strong enough." He broke down, unable to hold back his sobs.

Brock squeezed Daphne's hand as tears formed in her eyes, too.

"I'm so sorry." She closed her eyes but couldn't shut out the memory of Emma's bruised and broken body.

"She fell from one of the headlands not far from the resort," Greg explained. "I tried to grab her, but I wasn't fast enough. The ocean swallowed her. I swam for hours looking for her, but…"

"Oh my God," Brock muttered.

"I had just given a hiker a note and my last twenty bucks to meet you at Scorpion Anchorage. I don't even know if you ever got that note."

"I did."

"I'm surprised." Greg sipped his water, trying to collect himself. "It was a long shot."

"I tried to get my parents to go back," Daphne said. "I was after them for weeks to get help and go back, but they wouldn't."

"Don't go back there," Greg warned. "Don't ever go back."

She reached her campsite and unburdened the pack onto the picnic table. It didn't take her long to put up the tent and transfer her food into the storage box that came with the site. She hadn't eaten since morning, so she made herself a little lunch with her new Jetboil stove. She boiled two cups of water and added one of the pasta mixes and a can of chicken. She'd eaten this concoction before and knew it was good, but today she couldn't taste the food; she was too nervous.

Once she had finished eating, she washed out the mug to her stove and then went to scope out this part of the island. She stopped first at the Visitor's Center at the historic Scorpion Ranch House—which was nothing like the house at Christy Ranch but was, nevertheless, interesting with its display about the Chumash heritage and the island's plant and wildlife. Then she checked out some of the hiking trails. The open flatlands on this side of the island were easier on her body, but were less scenic. She'd been told by the woman at the Ventura office not to miss the sunset at Potato Harbor, so she followed the trail along the northern shore with a few other hikers and was pleased with the views once she came to the crest overlooking the sea. The spectacular scene uplifted her spirit, but as she headed back toward her tent, tears stung her eyes. That voice of doubt returned, repeating its mantra: *You don't know what you're doing.*

And the simple fact was, she didn't quite know what she was doing. Yes, she had a plan, but it was flimsy at best. Her "Plan A" was to kidnap Cam. She had brought rope, a gag, and chloroform, to help her. If she got caught, she would fall on "Plan B," which was to secretly capture as much video on her phone as possible, something to show the

FBI. In three days, Mrs. Turner would arrive with the police. Mrs. Turner had come with them once before, but Cam had refused to return with his mother, and since he was an adult, there'd been nothing she or the police could do about it; but Daphne didn't turn eighteen for another month. And there was no way, when asked, that she would ever tell the police that she wanted to stay on the island.

Her mind raced back to that afternoon with Greg at the café in San Antonio.

"The second thing I wanted to tell you was…Can you please get your parents to talk to the FBI? What my parents are doing over there, it's criminal. They've got to be stopped."

Daphne arched a brow. "Wait. *Parents? Both* of your parents are over there?"

"Who's your father?" Brock asked.

"Arturo Gomez," Greg answered. "I thought you knew that."

"You introduced yourself as Gregory Gray." Daphne looked back and forth between the two boys. "How could I know?"

So, Greg was Arturo's son. Daphne let that sink in.

"Well, he didn't know about me for the first seven years of my life," Greg explained. "It's a long story. My point is they need to be stopped."

"I've already asked my parents to talk to the police," Daphne said. "They won't. They're too grateful for what your mom has done for me and Joey."

Greg put his face in his hands.

"Why can't *you* go to the FBI?" Brock asked.

"I did—about four years ago. I got handed back over to my parents. No investigation. Nothing but a slap on *my* wrists."

"Why *your* wrists?" Daphne asked.

Greg lifted his brows. "Have you met my mother?"

"What makes you think Daphne's parents can have any better luck?"

"For one thing, they're adults," Greg said. "And for another, they aren't related to her."

"They won't do it. Believe me, I've tried," Daphne said. "If only we had some of the surveillance video, some evidence we could show the authorities."

"What's the third reason?" Brock asked Greg.

Greg bit his lip and squeezed his hands together. "I, uh…"

The waitress brought their plates and a bottle of ketchup. "Get you anything else?"

"No, thanks," Daphne said.

Once the waitress had gone to take the order of another customer, Greg leaned in and said, "I hate to ask this. But my third reason for coming was, well, I was wondering if I could borrow a few hundred dollars." Then he added, "I promise to pay you back."

"Of course," Daphne said, without hesitation.

"Do you have a job?" Brock asked.

"I did," Greg explained. "But if I'm going to have a steady job, I need to change my name, first, and get new identification, so my parents can't find me."

"But your trust fund…" Daphne started.

"You think I want their money? Do you honestly think I want anything to do with my parents?" Greg's eyes widened and he bounced up and down in his seat. "I'd kill myself before I'd take their money."

"Calm down," Brock said. "I get it."

As Daphne reached her tent and crawled inside of that tiny, suffocating space that would be home for the coming days, she felt more alone than ever. She needed to fall asleep so that when darkness came, she could pack everything up and sneak away from the campgrounds to the other side of the island. If she got caught crossing the fence by a park ranger or a conservancy officer, that would be the end of it. No one was allowed on the Nature Conservancy side without a permit. She'd looked into getting one, but she didn't have the training and experience required. Sneaking and breaking the law were her only options.

But if that's what it would take to save her best friend, and maybe all of the Calibans, she would do it. Greg had warned her not to come back to the island without the FBI, but that was before she had spoken to Cam's mom.

It had been early January. Daphne had come home from school. She'd parked in the driveway and was crossing the lawn, when Mrs. Turner appeared beneath the oak tree that divided their two properties.

"Hello, Daphne."

"Oh, hi, Mrs. Turner. How are you?"

Cam's mom folded her arms. "I'm okay, thank you. How about you, dear?"

"Good, thanks."

"By any chance, have you spoken to Cameron recently?"

Daphne shook her head. "Not since we left the island last summer. Why?"

Mrs. Turner's lips trembled. "I don't know how to get in touch with him. He stopped writing to me. He hasn't called, either."

Cam's mom had told Daphne last fall how upset she'd been when she'd learned Cam didn't plan to return to college. He had decided to stay and work for Dr. Gray.

"There's no cell reception there," Daphne said.

"He didn't come home for Thanksgiving or Christmas," A tear slipped down Mrs. Turner's cheek, and she swiped it away with a shaky hand. "I don't know what to do. I'm thinking about going back to the island and bringing him back."

After hours of tossing and turning without a wink of sleep, Daphne put on her headlamp and wrote in her poetry journal. None of the words seemed to flow properly for several minutes, but then she finally caught her rhythm and wrote:

I'm not a girl to be scolded, coddled, or patronized,
Or to be overlooked, tricked, or glamorized.
No Prospero rules me or my fate.
I'm my own island; I forge my own gate
To hell and back.
Call me Caliban, if you like, but this girl will rise
And blight you with her dragon flames and cries
For justice.

She reread the poem, and then, satisfied, put it away and hiked to one of two outhouses on the campground. It was a wooden structure with a non-flushing toilet, bio-degradable toilet paper, and hand sanitizer. The inside walls were covered in writing, worse than any bathroom stall she'd seen at her high school. Much of it was crude and obscene, but a lot of it was declarations of love, like *Lisa loves Richard* and *Jamshid and Marcy forever.* More than love, people seemed to need to declare their existence: *Sam was here, James was here, Jose was here, Paul was here, Trevor was here, Solomon was here, Shirley was here, Juan was here, Cathy was here, Atzimba was here,* and on and on, including *Greg was here.*

She almost fell in the toilet when, in permanent black marker, scrawled on the upper right corner of the door, she read:

Cam loves Daphne.

EVA POHLER

Eva Pohler is a *USA Today* bestselling author of over thirty novels in multiple genres, including mysteries, thrillers, and young adult paranormal romance based on Greek mythology. Her books have been described as "addictive" and "sure to thrill"—*Kirkus Reviews*.

To learn more about Eva and her books, and to sign up to hear about new releases, and sales, please visit her website at www.evapohler.com.